Rescued by a Kiss

First in the Series
The New Orleans Go Cup Chronicles

Colleen Mooney

eBook ISBN-10: 0990552705
eBook ISBN-13: 978-0-9905527-0-3
Print ISBN-10: 0990552713
Print ISBN-13: 978-0-9905527-1-0

Cover design by Kari Ayasha and Cover to Cover Designs

Dedication

"A dog is the only animal that will love
someone more than it loves itself."

Anonymous

Dedicated to rescued dogs and Schnauzers
everywhere, in particular the ones who left paw
prints on my heart, Cricket Ann, Madchen
Mooney, Kugel, Tara Strudel, Schnitzel, Schatz,
Earhart, Meaux Jeaux Mooney, MoonPie Mooney,
Mauser the Schnauzer, Frederick and Tweezer.
Special thanks to those of you who have opened
your hearts and homes to help me rescue them,
because without you, I'd have 1,000 dogs!

Acknowledgements

I wish to thank Sandra Faught, Kathy Rush, Danielle Carigan, Susan Spencer, Denise Alix, Martha Good, Terrie Savoie, Lucy Michael, Fritz Zeigler and Terrie Valdes for their time, encouragement and feedback on my manuscript. Thanks to Eileen Casey, Blair Schmidt and Blair Casey who helped with the cover, and Colin and Ashley Casey for their moral support.

Thanks to Judy Bruzeau of Pet Palace, Susan Diehl, Lake Animal Hospital and Staff, Algiers Animal Clinic, Fetch! Mid-City, Animal Care Hospital, Southern Animal Foundation and my foster families who support, volunteer their time, love and hearts to Schnauzer Rescue's mission. Their big hearts and dedication makes it possible to rescue and place more dogs than I could ever do on my own.

In addition, a special thanks to my husband, Bill Cope, who thinks and tells everyone that I can do anything. I love his never ending support for Schnauzer Rescue and me.

Go Cups, or Geaux Cups are plastic cups stacked at the end of all bars in New Orleans near the door. They are for patrons to empty what is left of their alcoholic drinks and take it with them. This allows the party, your friends and drinks to move with you.

Chapter One

THE NIGHT OF the shooting was a good one to catch pneumonia, but instead of staying home, I was at a Mardi Gras parade trying to catch beads. Julia took out a bottle of wine and two plastic wine glasses from her enormous leather shoulder bag and poured a drink for each of us. Suzanne, my childhood friend, held out a plastic go cup she just caught off a float for Julia to pour some wine into.

I was in my four-inch heels, and was still about six inches shorter than Julia. She had Dallas hair and wore big flashy gold and diamond jewelry, all of which were real. She took an inordinate amount of time to make sure her outfit was 100 percent coordinated, accessorized, pressed, or steamed. She spent forever getting dressed. It took her an hour to put on her makeup, and another hour to make sure her hair was just the right height. A wedding took less preparation than it took Julia getting ready to go, well . . . anywhere.

Julia purchased what nature failed to deliver.

Those guys up on the floats looking down Julia's blouse were in for a treat. She was a stunner before her recent boob job, or, as Julia referred to it, augmentation. Now, all heads were turned toward her, all except my mother's. "Suzanne, you wanna drink outta something that has been rolling around on the ground before you wash it?" Julia hesitated for about a blink before pouring. Julia's Baton Rouge accent added an "r" to wash making it sound like 'warsh'.

"The booze will kill any germs," Suzanne answered, seemingly unfazed.

"What doesn't kill you makes you stronger," I toasted, and we bumped glasses.

My name is Brandy Alexander, and I am twenty-six years old still living at home with my parents. I'm tall, thin, and God gave me the girly attributes Julia had to pay for. My hair is shoulder length, straight, and blonde. I wear it down or pulled into a ponytail on top of my head. I love King Cakes, and I'm a sucker for an abandoned dog, especially if it's a Schnauzer. Dad says these dogs find me; it's in my aura. And, just ask my Mother; I'm personally responsible for everything that goes wrong in the world and at home. She's Catholic, southern, and responsible for my biggest phobia, the cockroach. And, here in New Orleans, they fly at you.

I live in a New Orleans neighborhood known

as the Irish Channel, and a relative or lifelong friend lives in every home on our block. I have known the family of five boys who live next door to us since I was born. Dante is a year older than me, and we have been childhood friends and pseudo-sweethearts since we could crawl. Both our families expect us to set a date for the wedding any day.

It was the first parade of the Mardi Gras season, and I stood with family and friends in the same spot where we had watched parades for the last twenty-six years. My boyfriend, Dante, is a New Orleans cop. He and his partner always arranged to get their police parade assignments at either end of the block closest to this spot. Everyone came out and stood near them for protection. The only protection any of us needed was from each other.

Between the floats and bands, the members of the gentlemen walking clubs, often inebriated, marched along. Their objective, fueled with liquid courage, was to coerce a girl for a kiss in exchange for a flower they carried with them on a walking cane. It was lighthearted foolishness. The gentleman got a kiss, sometimes a peck on the check, or the fella kissed a girl's hand presented in exchange for a homemade paper carnation. These kiss-flower negotiations were nothing serious—except with the man I kissed. New Orleans parades provide a decadent experience for every one of the senses. Bands passed, and their bass drums pounded in my chest. Vendors pushed carts of candied apples, cotton candy, peanuts, corn dogs, and popcorn. Smells of swirled cotton candy and peanuts mingled with whiffs of whiskey and marijuana from the crowd as they played, bumped, and pushed into each other and me. The yelling, laughing, and screaming died down after each float passed. When I looked back to the parade, my eyes locked onto those of a man with black, piercing eyes, a swimmer's body, and James Bond good looks. He was standing still and staring at me. I have a weakness for the tall, athletic type with a great tan. The formal wear was a bonus.

He wore a tuxedo like all the club members and he stood in the middle of the street, not at the curb working the women for kisses. He didn't have a drink or carry a cane of flowers. He held a few paper carnations in one hand. His confident demeanor and blatant attention caused me to catch my breath.

We stood there looking at each other for what felt like an eternity. I have no idea how much time passed from this moment on.

I knew I was going to kiss him. He never waved or gestured for me to come over. He just stood there, staring. He never took his eyes off me. No one had ever looked at me with such intensity.

I didn't remember handing my glass to Julia. I didn't remember my feet moving. I glided in a trance. Some invisible force locked onto me and transported me to him, into the street, the noise, the music, and yelling—away from my parents, friends, boyfriend's parents, and Dante. I moved along a straight line in the direction of his face. People moved out of my way without bumping or touching me.

Everything around me—people, noise, music—faded away. I felt alone with him in the middle of St. Charles Avenue. Everything went silent as I glided up and stopped toe-to-toe, face-to-face with him, in the middle of a parade with people teeming all around us. In our quiet space, I could hear him breathing. I could smell him, not his cologne . . . him. The way he smelled made my skin tingle. He never unlocked his eyes from mine as he put his right hand around my waist and pulled me into him. I ran my hands up his arms and rested them on his shoulders. He moved his face to me and put his mouth on mine. Our bodies melted into each other, a perfect, comfortable fit. I don't know how long it lasted. It was long, slow, hot—unlike any kiss I have ever had in my life.

My right leg bent up at the knee all by itself. I don't know how long I stood there in the street, in a bubble, in the kiss, on one foot. It could have been a minute or an hour. Everything stopped. We were alone in a world that belonged only to us. The rest of the parade—bands, floats, revelers, everything—just disappeared.

Then, I felt his face moving away from mine. He placed his warm giant hand behind my neck to turn my head. His lips brushed my ear and he whispered, "Meet me at the end of the parade."

His warm breath in my ear sent a heat wave down to my toes. As our faces moved apart, he pressed all the flowers he held into my hand with the intensity of his look. The kiss ended and the parade, with the thousands of people and noise, began to fade back into my awareness. The sounds and movement crescendoed until it resumed its original pitch. I could hear a policeman saying to him, "OK, lover boy, let's keep it moving, before I have to call a fire truck." The same policeman said to me, "You have to get behind the curb, Miss." He moved The Kisser along, grabbed my elbow and guided me to the curb. I knew the cop's voice and he knew my name. Why was he calling me "Miss?" I looked around as I left the bubble. The voice belonged to Dante's partner, Joe.

When I got back to my spot standing next to Julia, my mother leaned over and said to me, "Brandy, you made a spectacle of yourself." What an accomplishment—since my competition was a Mardi Gras parade. Then she turned and walked back to stand with my dad. Dad was smiling at me until my mother gave him the look.

"Brandy, are you OK?" Suzanne asked. "You look like Dante popped you with his stun gun."

"Yeah, yeah. I'm fine."

Julia started prying to find out what he said in my ear. I told her. Ignoring the disapproving looks from my mother, Dante's parents, and all the neighbors who came to the parade, I decided to meet him. Normally, I don't believe in a kiss at first sight. But, as I was drawn into the street for the kiss, I felt similarly drawn to go to the Municipal Auditorium where the parade would end to find him. Dante didn't look at me. I had already forgotten his instructions from earlier in the evening to go straight home after the parade. He told me the police had it on good authority that there may be problems tonight with the crowd.

I had to find out why I had connected so intimately and without hesitation with the man I had kissed—in front of a thousand people, no less. I couldn't blame my actions on drinking. I didn't taste liquor in his kiss and Julia took my untouched plastic flute from me when I started moving to the street. What are friends for, if not to hold your drink while you make a spectacle of yourself?

Before the last float approached, Julia and I left so we could make it to the Municipal Auditorium, where the parade would disband. Where the parade ends always looks like a scene right out of a Godzilla movie, with the Japanese fleeing the monster in mass hysteria. The traffic, people, animals, police cars, floats, bands, equipment and riders all scrambled. Everyone was pushing, shoving, and cursing to get to the next party, a carnival ball, or home. A free-for-all didn't begin to describe it.

I found him. I found him right away. The necktie he wore with the tuxedo hung untied around his neck. He looked at me at the same time I spotted him and he broke into a heart-melting smile. He was even better looking when he smiled. I couldn't stop the heat rising up my body to my face or the smile I felt spreading from ear to ear. He was walking away from me at a 45-degree angle, and without losing a beat to change direction his next step moved in the direction of my face. This was easier than I thought. It felt as if the cone of silence that enveloped us while kissing was going to work again.

Julia stood right next to me and pointed over my shoulder saying, "There he is!" She sounded as if she were off in the distance.

Our eyes remained glued on each other as he continued making his way toward me. Again, I didn't need to push and shove. People just moved out of the path we made to each other. As we came face-to-face, we both reached out our hands to take the others. Just as we touched hands, and before I could even ask his name, or tell him mine, a shot was fired. The sound of the gun exploded next to my head.

Everyone went berserk, running into us from every direction. We never lost eye contact as he went down to the ground. When he pulled me to my knees along with him, I saw the blood all over his shirt. He pulled me in close to his face, squeezed my hands and gasped, "Please, help me. Please save Isabella." Then he passed out.

The police were everywhere.

Chapter Two

I HADN'T EXPECTED that night to spin out of control the way it did. It had started out like any other Friday after work. I planned a quick stop by the animal shelter to drop off some newspapers on my way home. Besides dropping off the papers, I made a pickup, which wasn't uncommon for me. I couldn't look the other way, especially for a sad dog no one wanted. Dealing with another dog was going to make me late to meet my friends for the parade and I had to sneak it past my mother.

"Shhhh. Stay quiet now," I whispered to the little dog inside the pet carrier. The car door seemed a lot bigger when I put the dog crate in here at the shelter.

I was leaning into the car, struggling with the crate, when a man leaned over me and I felt his breath on my neck. "You should try to be more stealthy if you don't want to get caught," he said as he grabbed me around the waist.

I spun around ready to start punching when I realized who the voice belonged to. "Dante, you scared me, I almost screamed." I never noticed his squad car parked there when I had pulled into our driveway. Dante's stealthiness and equanimity came courtesy of U.S. Military training. If you asked him exactly what he did on his tour, he changed the subject or flat out ignored the question and then walked off.

"Do you want my mother to see me with another dog?" I started struggling with the dog crate again.

"Really, Brandy? She is going to see it and hear it," he said. "You live in the same house."

"Why are you home anyway? Did you lose your parade?" I asked, annoyed that he didn't try to help me with the crate. He stood there and watched me wrestle it out of the car.

He waited until I gave him my undivided attention as we stood face to face with the dog crate between us. "We got a lunch break after ten hours of work and I'll probably work another ten hours, so I came home to change into a clean uniform. I'll see you at the parade in the usual spot, but come straight home after. I can't meet you tonight. At roll call we were briefed to stay on another two hours after the parade. At roll call, the Lieutenant said they are expecting trouble and they want us on duty in case it goes down."

His tired face leaned into mine and kissed me on the check. "You smell like King Cake," he said.

"Randazzo's?"

"Yes, I passed it on the way home and have two in the front seat. Want some?"

"It only looks like one and a half King Cakes. You've been sampling?"

"Just doing a quality control check to make sure it meets my King Cake standards, and I gave some to Fido here to make friends. He was hungry." I leaned in and broke off a chunk for him to take with him. When I came out of the car he was holding the crate, so I stuck the King Cake in his mouth and he transferred the carrier to me.

"I gotta run," he said, chewing. "I'll see you at the parade. Maybe tomorrow night we can grab a bite." He walked off and got in his squad car. As he drove away, he leaned out the window, turned the police search light on me and announced over the loudspeaker, "Brandy Alexander go straight home. Remember what I told you."

The entire neighborhood heard what my marching orders were. The back door to the house creaked and I couldn't hold it open and get the crate in at the same time. I was struggling again when it flew open and there stood our housekeeper of the last umpteen years.

Woozie held the door with one hand, the other on her hip, pressing her back to the frame to allow me to squeeze past. "Oh Sweet Jesus, you done brought home another stinky dog. Your mama gonna pitch a conniption fit."

"Shhh," I was trying to keep Woozie quiet. "I'm trying to get this guy in and cleaned up before she sees it."

"Brandy, your mama got eyes in da ceiling, and des walls are paper thin. Everybody hears everything about everybody else in this house. She already knows you got dat dog. Thank Gawd I'm finished for today and needs to catch me da Magazine bus before all you crazy people going to da parade get streets shut down." Woozie was a true 'Yat' and pronounced most words starting with 'th' with a 'd'. This, that, these and those sounded like dis, dat, dese and dose.

"I'm supposed to go to the parade too, with Julia. I'm late 'cuz I had to go get this little guy."

"Cuz you had to get another dog?" Woozie tipped her head side-to-side with every word mimicing me.

"He was left tied to the fence outside the shelter. I couldn't leave him there or I'd have nightmares."

"You gonna be living with the nightmare once your mama sees him." She stood at the bottom step and nodded toward the living room where my mother was. Woozie blew me a kiss. "I read da cards for your mama and in dere was one with your name on it. The Tarot said, 'Brandy, stay home.' You should stay home tonight or you might catch your death of cold. Good luck with dat mutt." She left with the big shopping bag she carried around with her like a purse. Woozie lugged it around with her everywhere she went. The only thing I ever saw her take in or out of the shopping bag was a deck of Tarot cards.

Woozie read the Tarot every time she came to clean. It seemed she made up the predictions depending on what was happening that day. If we doubted something in the cards, she pulled out a crystal on a silk cord and let it circle around a few times by way of confirming her reading. While none of us put any stock in Woozie's superstitions, we minded not to tell her as much.

I hoped her comments about the dog were being drowned out by the ruckus at the front of the house. Someone was hammering away on the front door and it set the dogs off barking while I tried to sneak in the back. Maybe my mother hadn't heard us. From the hall I could see the drama unfolding in the living room.

"Come in, it's open," Dad bellowed from his Lazy Boy command center over the yapping dogs.

Julia entered in broadcast mode and could be heard throughout our house. I stood in the hallway and tried to get Julia's attention without alerting my mother. Julia fired off questions, asking how they were, were they going to the parade, was I home yet and was this all the dogs I had rescued?

Her questions ran together like they were all somehow related. She asked the dogs questions, too, and didn't wait for anyone to answer her. "Get back, you little wild Nicki Hokies. I'm not chasing you up the street in these four-inch heels. Gawd, it is cold tonight." She stood five foot eleven inches before you added the four-inch heels and big hair.

Julia and I had worked together in sales at the phone company until a month ago when she was laid off. When I asked her what was a Nicki Hokie she responded it had to do with her Indian heritage and that was her tribe. Her outfits, too tight, too low cut, and too short for my mother's approval, always met my dad's. Tonight's ensemble was a combination of animal prints. She looked like Peg Bundy slammed into Chris Owens on Bourbon Street. I tried to get Julia's attention.

"If you covered your chest in clothes made for this weather you might not be so cold," my mother admonished Julia. My mother expressed her dissatisfaction with a look that could cut through cinder block. Julia ignored her. Seeing them spar reminded me of lady wrestlers circling each other vying for the best position to strike.

"If I covered my assets, I wouldn't catch any beads. Y'all going to the parade with us?" Julia asked my dad, as she glared at me standing in the hall holding the crate.

"Brandy parked in the back. I heard her sneaking in the back door with another dog when Woozie left," my mother told her. Except for vital exchanges of information or a chance at a backhanded insult, my mother and Julia ignored each other.

Great, she knew. So much for the element of surprise, I thought.

"C'mon, I need to change before we leave," I said to Julia. Dad got up and followed saying, "You two better step on it. I just saw the trouble truck through the front window go by right before you knocked." Dad took his self-appointed job as parade monitor seriously. From his Lazy Boy Operations Post in front of the Camp Street window, he could see when the parade's trouble truck passed. Spotting this truck allowed him to announce the parade's estimated time of arrival. The trouble truck, outfitted with a pole indicating the tallest point of the parade, assessed overhead clearance for the floats to pass safely along under a tree, power line, or bridge. Once the truck passed, the parade was just minutes away. At any moment we would hear motorcycle sirens blasting, clearing people out of the street to make way for the beginning of the parade. We would have to hurry to get there for the start of it.

My apartment sat in back of the main house down the hall from the living room, and shared the side entrance. Julia said it was within "snooping distance" of my mother so she could hear me change my mind. Dad and Julia checked out the dog.

Julia gushed over the furry black ball while the dog wiggled in her arms. Then she held him out at arm's length. "He kinda stinks," she put the dog down and looked for somewhere to wash her hands. "His hair looks like dreadlocks. Why don't you name him Bob Marley? Are you sure he is a Schnauzer?"

"Yes, he's a Schnauzer and his name is . . ," I said trying to think of one.

"Go Cup," my dad finished for me. "With a name like Go Cup your mother will think he won't be here long. You girls get going to the parade. I'll take care of this little guy." He continued to give the dog a vigorous head petting. "Boy, you do stink but you can't help it, can you? I'll get you cleaned up."

"Go Cup is all right, I guess, but spell it G-e-a-u-x instead of Go," I said. "I'd planned to bathe him, but the parade traffic was awful. I found him tied to the fence outside the shelter."

My calling to do animal rescue came from Dad. He was always bringing home strays. When I was in sixth grade, Dad brought home a little black Schnauzer mix I named Cricket Ann. She lived with me for fifteen years. When she went to the

Big Milk Bone in heaven, I decided I wanted a dog as close to her size and personality as possible. At the shelter, there was a full-bred black Schnauzer that looked just like her. I named him Meaux Jeaux and he put paw prints on my heart the second I saw him. Meaux ruled over everyone in our house, even my mother who made overtures of disapproval when it came to the dogs. But I would see her sneak scraps to Meaux under the table during dinner.

"What are you wearing?" Julia asked, not waiting for me to answer my dad.

"I'll groom him when I get home if you'll bathe him," I said to Dad. "I'm wearing this," I said to Julia, stepping out the bathroom in a turtleneck and jeans.

"No, wear that scoop-neck sweater that shows some cleavage," Julia said.

"You know we can't keep another dog. Your mother . . ." Dad was trying to change the conversation back to the dog.

"I know. Four dogs are three over the limit." Raising my right hand up and placing my left hand over my heart, I made the pledge. "I will go on record and say I plan to find this one a home." To Julia I added, "I'm wearing parade colors," as I pulled out a purple sweater and stepped back into my bathroom to change into it along with the matching lace bra and thong underwear as well. If someone was going to look down my sweater, I wanted them to know I had fashion sense. I put on a jacket and zipped it up to avoid my mother's disapproving look on my way out the door.

"After you move into your own place you can rescue all the dogs you want," Julia said.

"Are you moving out?" Dad's head snapped up as he blurted out the question aimed at my bathroom door.

"Baby birds are supposed to leave the nest, right?" I said stepping back into my room making flapping movements with my arms in an attempt to amuse him.

"Well, I just thought you'd move out after you and Dante got married," he said looking back at the dog and not making eye contact with me. Julia gave me an eye roll and head nod toward the door.

"Well, I'd like to know I could make it on my own first. I've been thinking of getting an apartment, one that's dog friendly." I couldn't look at Dad. I didn't want to see the sad look in his eyes that matched the sound in his voice. We both knew it was high time for me to be making a life on my own. I needed to get out of my parents' home, but according to my mother, nice girls didn't move out until they were married. I hurried and said, "OK, Julia, let's go. Danielle and Suzanne are meeting us there, and they're saving us a good spot on Lee Circle." I didn't want Dad asking any more marriage questions.

"Try not to get into trouble or bring home any more dogs," my mother said as I kissed her goodbye.

Nodding his head toward my rear apartment, Dad said, "Your Mother and I will meet you in our usual spot. You girls go on now and don't worry about . . ."

"The stinky dog," my mother said finishing his sentence. "I guess you better feed it along with the other three after you bathe it. What did you name it?"

Outside, I picked up our pace to adjust to the chill in the damp night air. Woozie was right. It was a good night to catch a cold and to stay home. My parents' house was one block off St. Charles Avenue, the major Mardi Gras parade route. We crossed the street and walked past St. Teresa's Church. All of us, my sister, Dante, all Dante's brothers, all the families on the block, had made our First Communion, Confirmation, and saw each other there every Sunday at Mass.

I heard the thunderous approach of the motor-cycle escorts. They revved their engines and it sounded like they were only a couple of blocks away.

"You know Dante will be there on St. Charles Avenue at Lee Circle. He arranges his parade assignment so we can watch the parade together," I said.

Julia did an eye roll that made her look like she was going into a coma. "He gets himself assigned where you tell him you're going to meet your friends so he can keep an eye on you. He's on duty, so he's watching for criminals or listening to that chatter from the radio in his ear. You're in the same place at the same time. Big difference. You get to speak to him in between radio talk? Sounds like fun. Between him, your dad, and your mother, you are never going to get laid."

"Dante is just right for me."

"Don't you mean just right next door? Didn't look too far for Mr. Right, did you? You should be looking for Mr. Show Me The World not settling for Mr. Right Next Door."

Ouch. Just for that I will wait until the end of the night to tell her she missed a loop with her belt at the back of her pants. In retrospect she will think her night was ruined.

She looked around the crowd and added, "I don't see my friends from work."

"Work? Which work?" I asked. After Julia had been laid off from the phone company she found work at The Club Bare Minimum in the French Quarter as an exotic dancer. This was information my mother never needed to know.

"I have other friends, you know, not just danc-ers from my current occupation. You should try the night club dancing scene. You might like it. We make great money in tips. Ask Suzanne."

"I should take my clothes off and dance naked in front of men for money?" I asked, with as much seriousness as I could muster.

"It's sounds bad when you say it like that. It's a better workout than going to the gym, and I make a few hundred a night. Besides, it would be fun to see your mother go over the edge."

We pushed through the crowd that swelled in the street, overflowed onto the sidewalks and up the steps of Lee Circle. We found Suzanne holding a place for us.

"I'm glad you made it" Suzanne said, smiling. "I was worried you were gonna miss the parade. It's a big crowd tonight. Everybody and his dog is here. Dante told us you brought home another one."

The busybody hotline was working overtime. My business was on the street before me. Julia was right. I needed to get my own place.

The Flambeaux carriers danced up the street while they twirled poles of fire. The tradition started when floats were drawn by mules or horses instead of trucks with generators. The carriers wrapped their heads and hands in rags to protect themselves from spewing kerosene as they danced and spun the poles. The crowd tossed them money for the entertainment. The real skill required the carrier to bend over in the street, pick up the quarters and not drop or spill kerosene into the crowd or onto the carrier in front of them. Even with all its possibility for calamity, I hoped this was a tradition that would never disappear or be replaced.

Julia said, "Their dancing, if you can call it dancing, is obscene."

This from a pole dancer? I spotted Dante and waved to get his attention. We made eye contact and I blew him a kiss. He smiled a weary smile until he noticed Julia and the smile faded into his work face. The police worked sixteen-hour days for two to three weeks until Carnival Season ended.

Police vehicles blasted sirens urging people to get behind the curb. Immediately after they passed, like water seeking its own level, the crowd flowed back into the street. Revelers danced, drank, and boys carried girls on their shoulders to get a better view of the parade. Next came the mounted patrol. They rode shoulder to shoulder and spread across the street curb to curb. They followed the squad cars and blew whistles at the same people who just moved out of the cars' path and right into theirs. The horses pushed the same people behind the curb, again.

The Shriners' motorcycle escort thundered by next. Engines roared and revved, lunging forward to keep the open spaces in the parade short. On the sidewalks, vendors pushed along carts of roasted peanuts and cotton candy behind the crowd. The food smells intertwined and wafted in the air. Even with the combined smell of horses, motorcycles, and exhaust, the cotton candy and peanut aromas made sales over the noise of the sirens and whistles. I heard the St. Augustine Marching One Hundred High School Band before I saw them. The horn section wailed out their fight song to the crowd who cheered them on.

Julia's favorite part of the parade approached— the gentlemen's walking clubs. These organizations consisted of men—young men, old men, and all ages in between. Even though the parade rolled at 6:30 P.M., all the Mardi Gras Krewes or clubs started their day at 8 A.M. with a breakfast of Bloody Marys or champagne cocktails. The official start of the parade kicked off the real drinking.

That was when I saw him, when I kissed a man I didn't know as if he were leaving to fight a war.

Chapter Three

AS THE MEDICS swarmed in, I felt hands the size of frying pans squeeze me by the shoulders and move me away from The Kisser. We held on to each other until the burley police officer lifted me off the ground, pulling us apart, and placed me about six feet away, saying, "Don't go anywhere. We need to ask you some questions."

Faces loomed before me, in and out of focus, screaming for me to move out of the way, only I didn't hear anything. Ambulance lights flashed and police shouted orders into megaphones. The crash truck drove in close to pick up The Kisser. It looked like a silent movie in slow motion. He was gone in seconds and I didn't even know his name.

The police rhythm changed, indicating they were now on high alert, moving fast. They taped off the area where the shooting happened and pushed people back out of the way. The parade's ending, for the police, changed from the drudgery of getting off work and going home to the frenzy associated with a full-blown crime scene. More police cars were arriving than were leaving.

Even while I was stunned and trying to comprehend what happened, Julia was babbling and repeating "Oh my Gawd! Let's get outta here!" But, I was trying to decide what to do next.

That was when Dante found me. He grabbed Julia and me by our elbows and pulled us away from the scene. Anyone in our way moved aside as he cut a determined path through the crowd, dragging us along. His jaw was set and the veins in his neck bulged up bigger and bigger with every step. After all, he'd told me to go straight home after the parade.

He didn't say a word. Julia didn't say a word. She looked pale and small next to him. I tried to resist being dragged, but without success. Dante had a death grip on each of us.

"Wait," I screamed but he didn't hear me or pretended not to over the noise.

He pushed me into the front seat of a police car, then Julia into the backseat. He marched around the back of the squad car, got in the driver's seat and started it up. He threw the vehicle in gear, turned on the police light and barked, "Buckle up."

"Where are you taking me?" I said. "I need to get back there."

"I'm taking you home, and then I'm going back to work," he said hitting the door lock.

"Home? That guy just got shot."

"Yeah, and what are you going to do about it? Did you see who shot him?" he asked.

"Well, no, I don't think so, but that policeman told me to wait, and said he wanted to ask me some questions."

"I am the police. Remember?" he spit out. "I'll take care of that."

"Well, maybe I do know something, maybe I saw something. Maybe Julia saw something. Maybe we should do our civic duty and stick around to answer the questions."

"Maybe you should go home like I told you to in the first place, and not stick around to let whoever shot that guy see you two." His voice felt like a slap to my face.

I looked at Julia for backup, but she hunched down in the back seat, as if trying to look invisible. Then it spilled out, with more than an edge to my voice, "Quit telling me what to do. I've had a lifetime of it already. Who do you think you are, pushing me around?"

"Miss Yakety Yak in the back seems to understand the danger. Look at her, or rather, listen." He tilted his head toward the back seat, as if trying to hear Julia. "Cat got your tongue, Julia?"

"My car is back there. How am I going to get it home?" I tried to convince him to let me out of the car.

"I'll drive it home when I take the squad car back. Julia, stay with her tonight," he said over his shoulder. It was more of a command than a request. Julia just nodded. Dante pulled down the driveway right behind the green station wagon that belonged to Mom, out of sight from the street. He slammed to a stop at the side door to my apartment. He sat looking straight ahead and hit the all-door unlock to dismiss us. We got out and without a word, he threw the squad car in reverse and drove backwards out the driveway at about fifty mph. No goodnight peck on the cheek, no *I'll see you tomorrow*, no nothing. Just rubber burning and gravel flying.

"Thanks for the ride." I hollered, waving to the squad car spinning backwards into a turn, then tearing off up the street. If Dante had been nicer, I might have told him that the guy who was shot mentioned someone named Isabella.

"Well, that was fun," Julia muttered.

"You can speak. Guess the cat didn't get your tongue." I stood there a second wondering why Dante was alone and where his partner was. They weren't off duty yet. I rummaged in my purse, found the car keys and got in the driver's side of my mother's station wagon. "Get in. We're going to look for someone named Isabella."

Chapter Four

"WHAT ARE YOU doing?" Julia asked.

As long as I could remember, my mother drove this big avocado-green station wagon, the ugliest car on the planet. It just wouldn't die, except now, it just wouldn't start. I often thought I might have to bury one of my parents in it because it was going to be with us forever.

"What are you doing?" Julia asked again, a little louder.

"Be quiet before someone inside hears you and comes out asking why I'm taking the station wagon. We're going to the emergency room to find out who that guy is." Finally, the engine turned over. This thing hated me. My mission involved someone named Isabella. I was getting a queasy feeling in my stomach over who this 'Isabella' might be. I didn't want to mention this to Julia just yet.

Julia stood her ground. "I want to go on record saying that this is not, I repeat, N-O-T a good idea."

"You want to go on record? That's my line, and quit using it." I said. "Now, get in the car." I considered Julia to be my wingman. Dante said we were more like wing nuts. I thought cosmic forces must be causing Julia and I to experience role reversal. "I'm thinking my wing nut should be helping me, not trying to sabotage me, unless, you want him for yourself? Is that it?"

Julia was fidgeting, "No, no, besides, Dante said to wait here."

"Dante said to wait here? When did you start listening to Dante? Or any man, for that matter. And when, oh when, did you start thinking I should listen to Dante?" I wanted her, no, I needed her, to come with me. This situation scared me and excited me all at the same time. "I'm the voice of reason, remember? Not Dante, and we know, not you. Besides, I need you to help me. Now get in."

She opened the passenger side car door and stood there. "How are we going to find out which emergency room? He could be in any one of six hospitals."

"He has a gunshot wound. Dante says all gunshots go to Charity Hospital. Having a boyfriend that's a cop comes in handy. Besides, if we get to Charity, and he isn't there, we can listen to the police scanner at the ER entrance and pick up where they took him."

Julia started getting out of the car again. "Are you crazy? Charity Hospital? Do you know how dangerous it is driving around there, not to mention, parking and getting out of the car? Forget going in there. It's a war zone. If you don't go in injured, you'll get shot or mugged when you come back to your car, assuming it hasn't been stolen."

She had a point. The nursing staff in the emergency room wore T-shirts that read 'Charity Hospital Where The Life You Save May Take Your Own'.

"Julia, get in the car. We'll be fine. There will be a ton of police there. It's Mardi Gras and a shooting just happened."

She didn't move.

"Fine. I'll just go by myself." That did it. She got in and started taking off her jewelry and putting it all in her purse. She wore more bling than the Royal Family wore to a Coronation.

"Why do you wear all that jewelry at the same time? Aren't you afraid of it getting stolen?" I watched her out of the corner of my eye as she took off two large diamond rings, several gold bracelets, some with diamonds, her diamond earrings that were two carats, and another smaller, half carat earring. She wore multiple earrings in each ear.

"It's insured, and like these," she said as she removed her ankle bracelet with as many diamonds as a tennis bracelet, a tennis bracelet, and a necklace with a diamond the size of my big toe, "they remind me of Barry." She put each into its own separate blue-velvet pouch that closed with a drawstring. It all disappeared into her enormous shoulder bag.

"Barry? Isn't that the one whose wife ransacked your condo?"

"Oh, you're right. Now that I think about it, he was a spineless jellyfish that sent his wife to break up with me. He gave her the key or she found it, and she threw my makeup all over my bedroom. She left a message in lipstick on my mirror 'Leave Barry alone!' He sent me these after that episode. I think it was to say, 'I'm sorry, I have no backbone'." Julia was still removing jewelry.

"You know, it would take less time for cops to strip off all their weapons before going through a metal detector." I said.

"Funny. You're a riot. Remember who is helping who here." While she attracted a lot of men and dated nonstop, she didn't keep them long, but she always got great parting gifts. I often thought the men she dated were happy to get out alive, and a couple of baubles were worth it.

"Good," I said, "if anyone tries to give us trouble, hit them with your purse now that you have all those rocks in it."

With all her jewelry in the safety of her handbag that was the size of some people's carry on luggage, she looked around the station wagon as if she just realized what vehicle we were in and asked, "Why does your mother still drive this thing? She like antiques or something? I bet they don't even make anything this color anymore. Does she have a refrigerator that matches it?"

"I really don't know. If I had the money, I would buy her another car and send this one to a junkyard," I answered her while trying to negotiate the potholes in the streets that could take a car's front end out.

"Well, if you want this monstrosity stolen or if you get us shot, Charity's the place to go." She was doing a full body pat down of herself to see if she removed all her jewelry.

"See, I knew you'd come around to my way of thinking," I laughed as she gave me the evil eye.

Charity Hospital is the largest hospital with the best trauma and burn unit in the South. If you get shot, you want to go to Charity. They see more gunshots than a firing range. The number of people who shuffle through the place is staggering. It's like Grand Central Station with legal access to morphine. Charity is a public facility that treats everything: Orleans-Parish prisoners with self-inflicted wounds, the indigent, gunshot wounds, burn victims, car crashes of the variety where the jaws of life are required, and just about every other trauma humans can create for themselves or other humans.

We walked through the emergency entrance and into a hall lined head to toe with stretchers on both sides of the corridor. There were women in various stages of childbirth, all screaming for someone to help or attend to them. An intern walked from woman to woman asking without a lick of interest, "Did you wait until you started delivery to see a doctor for the first time?" He marked their answers on a chart.

A few stretchers further along the hallway sat a man with an axe stuck in the middle of his head. He sat facing sideways, feet hanging off the gurney, and looked at people passing. The axe was buried in his skull between his eyes and it made him appear cross-eyed when he looked at Julia to check out her boobs. Even an axe in the head didn't stop men from looking at boobs. The corridors were jammed with patients standing, sitting on the floor, or lying on stretchers moaning and writhing. A few grabbed at us for help. We had entered the Gates of Hell.

Two staff members in scrubs walked shoulder to shoulder down the hall making plans for when their shift ended, oblivious to the people suffering on stretchers lining their path. I was successful in maneuvering us down the hallway crammed with people on and off stretchers until we had to squeeze past these two. We stepped to the side allowing them to pass when a man leaning on the wall grabbed Julia asking, "Are you a doctor? Can you help me?"

"Dr. Julia is a sex therapist, but we will find you a real doctor," I told him and he, reluctantly, let go of her arm.

"A sex therapist? Is that the best you could do? Really? Tell the next one who asks that I'm a brain surgeon." I ignored her. Julia didn't have sympathy for the sick or injured as they took attention away from Julia.

I leaned into her hair and whispered in her ear, "I'm hoping all the confusion in this place will be enough of a distraction so we can find out who this guy is, and maybe even talk to him."

"Wow, you're trying to meet a guy who might be comatose, and you don't want me setting you up with anyone I know?" Julia asked amused.

We found an admission station, and I asked the very large woman with an RN badge if anyone had been admitted with a gunshot wound. Without looking up or stopping what she was doing, she asked, "Man, woman, or child? What time did they get shot?"

A child? I had heard all the horror stories from

Dante. I tried with a little more info, "Well, it was at the end of the parade tonight, one of the guys in the marching club got shot."

"Sorry, Sugar. Can't give out any information unless you are his next of kin," Nurse Camille Aucoin responded as if on auto pilot.

"My friend," pointing over at Julia standing by herself looking around and checking out her surroundings as if lost, "is his sister. Someone called her and told her to come down here. She's very distraught. I'm a family friend, and I'm just trying to help her find her brother."

Still looking at the chart in her hand, RN Aucoin said to me, "Well, he would'a been put in that hall on a stretcher down on the right. He might be in surgery already. After surgery he'll get moved to a room or stay in ICU if he isn't stable." She looked up from her clipboard and said, "He needs his next of kin, your friend, to stay here and fill out some information for him."

"Of course, after she sees her brother I will get her right back here to fill out any forms you need. Thank you for your help, Miss, uh . . . Nurse Aucoin." I looked around for Julia to head down the hall in the direction she indicated with her head nod. Just as she was about to shout at me to take the paperwork, the phone started ringing and she took the call. It distracted her long enough for me to get away.

A police officer stood writing on a clipboard a few feet away from Julia. She took a deep breath, squared her shoulders flipped her hair back with one hand, and moved right up next to him. He was a young guy, late twenties, and as tall as Julia. He filled out a uniform that made you know he worked out, a lot. He and Julia had something in common, tight clothes. I could hear her asking in her flirty voice if he was the Captain who helped her friend, the one shot at the end of the parade. God, I hoped that nurse stayed on that call and didn't look up. He told her he was the one who brought him to the hospital, but he was only a patrolman. Bingo.

"You know, if his name's spelled wrong, the insurance company will hold up his money, and the poor fella already has been shot. Oh my gosh, can you imagine how his insurance claims will get all gummed up?" She removed the clipboard from him checking to make sure the victim's name was spelled right. This guy was putty in Julia's hands even if he did have a gun. I started moving away just as I heard the cop trying to impress Julia, by telling her he pulled the name and address right off his driver's license. "Does it all look right to you, Miss Uh? How are you related to the victim?" he asked. She was on her own.

I moved down the hall looking for the third stretcher when someone grabbed me from behind and spun me around. I stood face-to-face with Dante and his partner Joe.

"What are you doing here? How did you get here?" The shocked look on Dante's face must have been a mirror image of what my face felt like seeing him. He leaned into me like a drill sergeant on a new recruit. We stood nose-to-nose as he waited for an answer. Julia walked up behind them and stopped dead in her tracks.

"I walked in. It was kinda easy," I said leaning backwards trying to recapture my personal space.

"Julia's rubbing off on you, and that's not a good thing. Let me ask you again. What in the hell are you doing here? Why didn't you stay home like I told you?"

I stammered, "I, I thought the police wanted to question us?"

"If the police wanted to question you, it would be at the station, not roaming around in Charity." Dante usually didn't have a temper, but he was hot. He hadn't seen Julia yet, and if he started dragging me to another squad car I would have two cars to get home, one being my mother's. I needed to get away from him.

Julia, overhearing the conversation, gave me the thumbs up signal—mission accomplished. I said, "OK, I'll go home. I was worried about you and wanted to make sure you didn't get hurt, too."

He didn't buy it. When I reached around him

and pulled Julia from behind, his eyes grew wide, his fists clenched, and his entire body tensed. Julia and I made a fast walking retreat toward the exit. Dante followed us all the way out the emergency room exit into the street and stood watching us make our way to the car.

"I've never seen him so ticked off at you," Julia said.

"Me either."

"I saw Dante and his partner when they spotted you. They didn't notice me, but his partner, Joe, isn't that his name? He saw you first and nudged Dante to point you out."

"Really? He had to know that would set Dante off."

"I think Joe intended to set Dante off, and I wonder why. C'mon, let's go get killed on the way to the car." I saw Dante in the rear view standing in the street watching until we rounded the corner.

Chapter Five

WHEN WE WERE clear of the hospital and Dante, I demanded, "OK, out with what you know. What did you find out?" I kept my eyes on the street, watching all around us as we made our way out of Charity's DMZ.

"He is one of the Heinkels. Big oil family, and they own most of the oil leases in Placquemines and St. Bernard Parishes. Think, 'The Shah of South Louisiana.' They have beaucoup money, and I think they're German. They're all attorneys: Jiff, Jason, Jake, Jimmy, and Jeffrey Heinkel. All their names start with a J; I think there's a Jared, too. The dad lives on Audubon Place Uptown, you know the street. It's the one across from Audubon Park with all the big mansions, big wrought iron gates, and security guards. That's guards, with an 's', as in plural. You hit the jackpot, girlfriend. Daddy Heinkel is a big hot shot attorney and all his sons work at the firm. They have been in the newspapers over oil lease disputes with some crackpot hustler down in The Parish."

"You found all this out from that cop's clipboard?" I asked.

"Nope. I recognized his name when I saw it."

"Julia, you know this guy? What's his name, Jiff or Jeff or one of the others?"

"Jiff. I don't know what it is short for, but that's what was on his driver's license, so it must be his God-given name. He would be your love interest. I know his daddy's name is Jeffrey Heinkel. Besides, how is this going to work with him being German and you being Catholic? Aren't Germans Protestant?"

"What kind of disputes? Germans can be Catholic. What does that matter? God help me."

"Jeffrey Heinkel, the Daddy, is the gentlemen I met. They've been in all the papers, even on TV. Did you see any of that stuff? His son, your Prince Charming, works at the firm. About two days ago I heard on WWL radio the Heinkel firm was involved in a parish-wide controversy over inherited oil leases, theirs, and little old ladies they represent. The guy trying to finagle the leases away from those old folks is using a little muscle to do it, or so they said on the news. Too bad he's not Italian, 'cuz they're all Catholics, right?"

Dante must have known who got shot, and who the Heinkel family was, and why me being there acting like I knew him could get me in a world of trouble. It sort of explained his road rage behavior.

"So, what's their address on Audubon?" I asked.

"I don't know, I just know the Dad lives on Audubon Place because he took me there one night. I met him and his wife at the Pontchartrain Hotel Piano Bar late one night after work. They bought me a drink and we talked for a couple of hours. They are both very charming. Then we went back to his house on Audubon Place for a nightcap. He had his limo driver wait and take me back to my car and then followed me home. He's a dying breed. It's called a gentleman."

"You met that guy before? Why didn't you tell me? Why did you let me go to Charity looking like an idiot?"

"I didn't meet the guy you kissed. I met his father. Aren't you listening? Since I didn't know who got shot until a few minutes ago, I couldn't know who he is or who he is related to. You know, you'd make a terrible detective. You better keep selling phones." She looked at me with her face all screwed up as if she wondered how I made it through a day by myself.

I took three deep breaths before I got my heart rate under control. Trying to interrogate Julia is an art form I haven't mastered. After a few deep inhales and exhales, I asked, "So, what is the address the cop had on our victim, the Heinkel that got shot? Jiff, right?"

"Oh, his address. He lives in the Tower Apartments, the real nice ones, on the Lakefront."

I mentally started mapping our route toward the lake.

"I can see what you're thinking, and we can't go there. Whoever shot that guy might be there. Or the cops might be there. Or, Mr. Right Next Door might be there with his partner, the snitch." Julia snickered.

She was never going to let that go. "That's exactly why we're going there, because Mr. 'Just-Got-Shot' asked me to do something for him." I didn't want to tell her he asked me to help someone named Isabella. It occurred to me there might be a screaming, ticked off, Italian girlfriend when Julia and I showed up and told her I kissed her boyfriend and then I saw him get shot. I shook my head to clear the thought.

Not having all of her jewelry on began to wear on Julia's patience. She hated to be out in public so naked and undressed. When her ensemble missed a vital accessory, she became irritated. All of her jewelry now resting in her purse must have her borderline manic.

Julia rummaged through her purse and asked, "What are we going to do, that the cops can't do? What did he ask you to do? Bring him a clean shirt? Water his plants? What?"

I plunged into what I knew would be met with some resistance, "He asked me to help someone named Isabella."

"Isabella! A woman! You are going to help his woman? It's probably his girlfriend, or worse, his wife." Julie sounded flabbergasted.

We were just two blocks away from Charity but still in the war zone. "Well, you can get out here and walk back to Charity and ask Dante for a ride if you don't want to go with me."

"Take the I-10," she said. "The parade traffic should be all cleared up, and that's the fastest way."

The Lakefront Tower is a high-rise apartment building with breathtaking views of Lake Pontchartrain from one side and downtown New Orleans, the Dome, and French Quarter from the other. It's very she-she-la-la, with its own doorman, like New York City apartment buildings. The doorman, Sam, is a friend and retired policeman who works as security there. I met him when he adopted a companion pet for his retirement. The dog turned out to be a Schnauzer under all the matted and stinky hair, much like the one back at home. Once groomed, he made for quite a good-looking, handsome dog and learned commands very fast. Sam and the dog quickly became devoted to each other. It made my heart sing to see them so happy together. Every time I ran into Sam at the grocery or bank he would tell me the dog's latest accomplishment. Sam was so impressed with how smart the little dog was, he named him Einstein.

When we got to the lobby I saw Sam on duty behind the front desk, and he smiled when he saw me. He took this job because he had a small apartment in the rear of the building, gratis, if he worked nights as security. That way he was never far from Einstein and could walk him or check up on him when he made his rounds.

We arrived at the Towers right after ten P.M. Sam opened the lobby doors which automatically locked at ten P.M. He let us in, and relocked them. If the police were there, they weren't in the lobby. After polite hellos I introduced Julia, also a dog lover. I asked if he had heard about the shooting at the parade. He said yes, but he didn't know who was shot. I told him that it happened to be one of the tenants, Jiff Heinkel, and Mr. Heinkel asked me before being taken to the hospital if I would come by to see if Isabella was all right. I had all my cards on the table, and I really hoped Sam would be as forthcoming about Jiff Heinkel as he had always been about Einstein.

"I'm so glad you know Mr. Heinkel. If he was shot, no telling when he will be coming home, and I'm happy, Brandy, to know you will help Isabella." Sam got the keys from behind the reception desk and headed to the elevator.

"Has Jiff Heinkel lived here long?" I asked trying to make small talk and get Sam to start giving up some information.

"Oh, a couple of years. He's been here ever since he graduated from Loyola Law School."

"Really. Do you know where he went to high school?" I asked.

"High school?" Julia burst into the conversation. "Why do you need to know where he went to high school?" I knew right then I would never take Julia on another covert mission.

Sam looked at Julia and asked, "You aren't from here are you?"

I jumped in and added, "If you know where a person went to high school, you usually know someone they know. That's how small New Orleans is. You get to know people better by finding out who you both know in common."

Sam looked at me, smiled and said, "It would be great if you could take Isabella home with you. C'mon, I'll take you up there and let you in."

Whoa Cowboy! I hoped he would let us into Heinkel's apartment, check and see if Isabella was okay, but take her home with me? My knees were getting rubbery just thinking what to say when I met her face-to-face. Julia allowed me to barge in without a well thought out plan. The amused smile on her face and her silence was annoying the hell out of me.

I prayed for enlightenment during the elevator ride. Sam put a key into a lock on the elevator panel and hit the button right above the twentieth floor that said, PENTHOUSE. Where else? I imagined meeting Isabella could go either way, however, I didn't expect her to roll out the red carpet for us. Enlightenment was slow to come; however, anxiety arrived at breakneck speed.

The elevator didn't stop. It just went straight to the Penthouse and opened directly into a vestibule. A wrought-iron enclosure acted as security outside the elevator for a front door. After leaving the elevator, guests had to be let into the apartment via the secondary wrought-iron door. Sam had that key too. As the gate opened without a sound, I heard a dog start barking. It appeared and ran toward us. It was a little salt and pepper Schnauzer. It ran right past Sam and up to me.

I thought, Isabella is going to be some kind of ticked off that we walked right in here and scared her dog.

Sam knelt down and lowered his voice when he spoke to the dog, "Now, Isabella, this nice young lady is going to take you home with her and take care of you until your dad gets better."

Isabella is a dog!

Kneeling down on the floor next to Sam to make friends with Isabella, I asked "Sam, doesn't

Mr. Heinkel, I mean, Jiff, have any friends, uh, lady friends, who might come for the dog?" I blundered forth, but Sam didn't seem to notice. Julia did. She nodded approval, encouraging me to get more intel on Heinkel.

"I wouldn't give this sweet little girl to any of those women. Half the ones who come around here looking for Mr. Heinkel he won't even let in. He makes me tell them he isn't home. I don't trust any of them anyway, at least not with Isabella. If you can't take her, maybe she can stay with Einstein and me until he gets home. He sure loves this little sweetie. So does Einstein. Einstein might not have Isabella's breeding, but they are both smart enough to recognize each other as fellow Schnauzers. Right Isabella?" Sam was rubbing Isabella's ears while she thumped her back foot in doggie bliss.

It's always interesting to watch a man with his dog or handle a gun. Both will tell you a lot about the guy.

"I can take her home with me, if it's too much trouble for Brandy to watch her," volunteered Julia.

"Oh, it is no trouble. I take in rescues all the time, and she's a Schnauzer. Isabella will fit right in with my dogs and get socialized at the same time," I said, cutting Julia off. *Great. Another yappy dog at home. My mother will be so happy.*

"Ok, let's find anything that's hers, like her food, a bed, toys and get going so Sam can get back to work." I smiled at Julia, happy over the fact that Isabella was a dog, and a Schnauzer, no less!

While the three of us rounded up Isabella's belongings I observed how inviting his condo was. Two big leather sofas faced each other and overstuffed chairs looked like you could sink into them, relax and enjoy his collection of local artwork. He had a very extensive library of books. His condo could have been done by a decorator. It was inviting, comfortable and elegant. Several photos of what looked to be his brothers with some of him and Isabella lined floor to ceiling bookshelves. Even with the masculine overtones, a woman would feel comfortable here. It felt like a home, not the typical bachelor pad. And he had a dog, a small, female dog, suggesting he didn't subscribe to 'my dog has to be an extension of my big, macho self.'

We found Isabella's doggie stuff, a bed, food, and a couple of toys when the elevator bell rang from the lobby. The doors closed and the button lit up as the elevator started its descent to the first floor. Sam went to the intercom and called the lobby. He had a puzzled look on his face and I knew why. Sam locked the lobby doors behind us after he let us in. Sam asked over the intercom,

"Security, can I help you?"

An inarticulate voice that sounded like it belonged to a large, not too bright guy came back over the box, "I was sent by old man Heinkel. I need to get some of his t'ings."

When Sam asked his name the guy responded angrily, "You don't need to know my name, you just need to let me in to get his stuff."

Then the elevator, with the key still in its panel unlocking access to the Penthouse, dinged and started up to our floor. Sam tried to raise the visitor on the intercom, but got no answer.

Chapter Six

"**S**AM, HOW DID he get into the lobby?" I asked. "You locked the doors behind us."

Sam moved fast saying, "Locks only keep honest people out and make the dishonest work harder to get in."

"I don't think that's a friend of Jiff Heinkel," I said.

"Or his Dad," Julia added.

"Sam, someone can walk right in here." He locked the wrought iron gate from the penthouse side saying, "This will slow them down, but not for long." He called on his police radio for backup. I scooped up Isabella. She looked at the elevator and started to growl.

Sam pushed Julia, Isabella and me into the kitchen and over to a door marked Freight. He unlocked it with a key. He shoved us into a room-sized dumb waiter that served all the upper floors for moving furniture or large deliveries in and out. Once we were inside, he closed a sliding metal accordion door across the opening and said, "This takes you to the ground floor behind the lobby. Watch your hands and feet. Be quiet and stay still until it gets to the first floor, then go out the emergency exit. The alarm will go off. Just get out of here."

I heard him calling in another 720 for police backup, when the service door closed and we started riding down to the basement. The chance of the police getting here anytime soon, on the night of a big parade, was not good.

Once the elevator started moving, the light went out. Julia, Isabella, and I sat in the dark riding down. Julia said, "I hope nothing crawls on us." Then we heard what sounded like gunfire. I worried about Sam. I realized we were sitting ducks in this elevator and not from bullets. Bullets I wasn't afraid of, OK, maybe a little afraid, but I was not nearly as afraid of them as I was of a roach. What Julia said put me in heart-racing, palm-sweating terror. I started breathing harder. Then, she had to add, "Well, if something does, you can't do anything about it. You will be like one of those feral cats caught in a Have-A-Heart Trap thrashing around. This elevator reminds me of those and I bet it's making you crazy."

Julia only made me dwell on my biggest phobia sitting in the dark with nowhere to go. My hands felt wet and my knees were rubbery. I thought of my last roach encounter. It was in my mother's kitchen two days ago, and I felt trapped there too.

I had put a glass in the kitchen sink when I saw him through the window moving up the back stairs straight for the open door. I had no way to stop him. I couldn't get to the door in time to close and lock it. My sister was in the habit of leaving the door wide open. It wouldn't have mattered, they had ways of getting in.

I moved back to the far side of the refrigerator hoping it would shield me from his view. I knew he could tell where I was hiding and could smell my fear. He began moving straight for me. I ran. I ran as fast as I could up the hall toward the living room. I couldn't outrun him. He flew after me, up the hall, closing in. I stumbled into the living room and fell behind the Lazy Boy where my father sat. Dad looked up, startled.

"Don't let him get me. Kill him. He's coming right at me!" I screamed, but no one rushed to help me. I froze, powerless to help myself. He was aiming for my face, moving at me, fast, very fast. "Stop him!" I gulped down breaths of air between sobs for help. "Please," I pleaded and grabbed my father.

"Really, Brandy? It's only a roach," my mother said. Her head didn't move. Her eyes peered over her glasses while she continued to sew rhinestones and sequins onto my sister's costume. She made no effort to move or come to my aid, and the costume needed to get finished for Sherry to wear on Mardi Gras.

"It's flying! Kill it . . . before . . . before . . . before . . . it lands on me!" I couldn't breathe and speak at the same time.

Rolling his Times Picayune newspaper into a make shift swatter my dad rose from his chair and gave my mother a disapproving look. He said, "This is all your fault. She wouldn't be like this if you hadn't terrorized her when she was a baby. You did this."

My mother would threaten me as a child by saying she would put a roach on me if I didn't take a nap, or be still, or keep quiet, or eat my food. She used it to make me do something I didn't want to do and she was determined to make me do it. It had a lasting impression. That was when I was two, and now its almost twenty five years later.

Dad swatted it to the floor. The roach ran under the sofa and he scrambled after it pushing furniture away from the wall to find the critter. He moved the sofa, then a chair and an end table before he stomped it into the afterlife declaring, "It's dead."

"You're wrecking my living room." my mother said.

"Are you sure it's dead? Did you stomp it? You need to stomp on it."

"Yes, I am sure it's dead." Dad was standing there watching the dead roach to see if it was going to move.

"I need to see it dead. You know, sometimes they play dead, and after you put them in the garbage can, later when you lift the lid, they fly out at you because they're pissed." I required confirmation to move on with my life.

"Well, come see," Dad said.

"Oh for God's sake," said my mother.

"This is all your fault," he repeated to her while I surveyed the roach's corpse. It looked enormous, at least a foot long, lying on its back with its big fuzzy legs folded stiff up in the air. "See what you've done?" he added.

"Next, she'll want you to call Dante to come put crime scene tape around the body," my mother said. My mother refused to take credit for the phobia she created. She feared nothing, except running out of sequins.

I pushed that memory out of my mind when we reached the basement and the dumbwaiter stopped. The very dim light bulb came back on and I looked around to make sure it was only Julia, Isabella and me in that cage. "I want out of here, please open the door." I blurted out even though my heart rate was getting back to normal once the light came back on. "Can you try? Can you try faster? I'm holding the dog."

Just then, the door slid open and there was Sam on the other side huffing and puffing. "I ran down the stairway when I saw this big fat guy trying to shoot at me through the iron gate." Sam didn't notice I almost knocked Julia off her feet pushing my way out the accordion door as he was opening it. He led us to the emergency exit, pulled out another key to turn off the alarm. He pushed the door open, pushed us out and said, "Be careful, and as soon as you can get to a phone, call the police." Then, he closed the door, locking us out and himself in.

Getting shoved around all night by men, even nice and well-intentioned ones like Sam, started to get on my last nerve. I just wanted to shove someone back, starting with the guy standing next to my mother's station wagon. We rounded the back corner of the building and came to an abrupt stop. We took a step backwards to hide from his view. He looked like a smaller version of the Lakefront Towers; a large, square block of a man. He faced the rear of the big, black, Cadillac with his slab of an arm slung over the open door, resting his fat stubby leg inside the frame of his car. He wore an ugly green warm-up suit that hung down to his knees in the crotch. It was almost the same color as my mother's station wagon. I wondered, *am I the only one who doesn't see the fashion sense in this color?*

He looked back and forth at the front lobby doors and up to the top of the building. He had parked right next to me, his car faced the street and mine faced the building. His car was positioned for a fast getaway. Mine was not. He stood in the door on the driver's side of his car, and I could not get into my car without asking him to move out of my way. I thought I heard police sirens in the distance. I'm sure some of the older, non-parade-going tenants called 911 when they heard the shots. Sam told me some of the old timers who lived in the building would call the police if anyone's dog pooped on the lawn.

We needed a diversion to get out of there and I wanted to avoid my third police confrontation at a second crime scene in one night. The way my luck was going, Dante would be first to arrive. I thought we should hop the back fence, and leave that blasted station wagon right there. The lobby doors flew open, the alarm sounded and the thug from upstairs lumbered out. He headed for the Cadillac. He wore the same ill fitting warm-up suit in red. He looked to be a scaled-down version of the driver wearing the green warm-up, but just as big, square, and dumb looking. The pair, dressed in matching red and green, looked like Santa's henchmen. I wondered why they weren't wearing the season's colors of purple, green, or gold. Red suit ran out of the building so he must have been the one who fired the shots. They wedged themselves into the vehicle and hit the gas. Green Fat Boy made too sharp a turn and caught his rear bumper on the bumper of the station wagon causing it to jack-knife behind the Cadillac. His car could not move.

He jumped out and lifted the station wagon off of their car. Impressive. I was really glad I did not run up and shove him.

Once he unhitched the two vehicles, he squeezed back into the Cadillac and went screaming out of the parking lot on two wheels.

Julia and I ran for the station wagon. We pulled out of the lot and turned in the opposite direction toward the New Orleans Yacht Club, and were half a block away dragging the front bumper when I saw at least five police cars in my rear view mirror turning into the Towers' driveway. I drove slowly as the bumper was dragging the ground causing sparks to fly up from the front end.

I rounded the bend out of sight of the Towers and the fleet of arriving police cars. I stopped to see if I could fix or tie up the front bumper. I found nothing in the car to use. Julia wriggled out of her bra from underneath her shirt.

"Here, use this. After my augmentation next week, I will need to buy larger bras. I won't be needing this size. Go big or go home, I always say."

Another augmentation? She was going to turn into the Bionic Woman. Time, being of the essence, I hooked the bumper to the grill wrapping Julia's bra around it twice and got us rolling again. Good thing she's a big girl.

I ran into the yacht club and called Sam. He answered on the first ring. "The police are here," he said. "I gave them the description of the two I saw leave the building. I'm not saying anything about you or your car in the report. I don't want them to find out who you are, and where you live, so I am leaving you out of it. They're sending over the crime lab to see if they can get ballistics from the shots fired and maybe an ID. Gotta run." He hung up.

The coast seemed clear, and I wanted to go back to Charity. I wanted to see Jiff Heinkel. I also wanted to tell him that Isabella was safe with me, and I wanted to tell him about the two thugs that tried to break into his apartment. A big part of me wanted to make sure he was going to be all right. If I got to kiss him again, well, I wanted to do that, too.

Chapter Seven

WHEN I GOT back into the station wagon, Julia's pager buzzed.

"Whose paging you?"

"Work. They're paging me to come in."

"What? I thought you had tonight off. Can't you get Suzanne to go in for you?"

"I did have it off, and Suzanne's already working tonight. I guess someone didn't show up, or it's really busy." Then she added with a hint of amusement at my predicament, "You could drop me at the club and I can get a ride home, or we can go back to your house to get my car. Chances are you will run into Mom and Dad. Oh, and then you can leave this dog there, too. Shouldn't you listen to your boyfriend, Dante, and go home?"

Julia could dance on my last nerve when she tried. If I took her to work, it gave me more time to figure out how to get back to Charity. I wasn't ready to go home and explain the kiss and Isabella just yet.

"Isn't this ironic after all the grief you give me

when I do listen to Dante? Let's talk about something else, like when you're getting divorced. On second thought, no, let's not." Julia didn't catch the edge in my voice and went off on another tirade.

I gave her a sideways look and headed back to the French Quarter across town. The parade would be over by now, but the crowds still partying would make it slow driving the Green Machine down Bourbon Street to Club Bare Minimum.

"If I had known he couldn't get it up, I wouldn't have married him," Julia started in.

"You, Julia, of all people, married someone without a test drive?"

She ignored me. "Come to think of it. He did get it up once. So we decided to try the pump. The doctor said it is perfectly natural for a man his age to have issues. S.J. wants to get a penile implant. Do you know how much those cost? Ten thousand dollars!"

I thought, *as much as a boob job?* She knew when she met him he was on the verge of bankruptcy and now she was surprised to find out he's sexually dysfunctional?

"So, we tried the pump. You know when a man is aroused, the blood goes into his penis and it starts to erect . . ." Julia started. I held up both hands to cut her off.

"Julia, stop. I know how a penis works in spite

of what you think about my love life. Continue. Go on about the pump."

She crossed her arms across her chest and stuck out her chin as if I had insulted her, then she picked up right where she left off. "Well, the penis goes in the acrylic cylinder at one end and I was supposed to pump it from the other end. You are supposed to see the penis getting bigger in the clear tube, and when it gets big enough you slip on a rubber band to hold the blood in to keep it erect. Well, I pumped it like the instructions said, and when it didn't get any bigger I called the 800 number on the tube, and . . ."

"Wait. What? You called an 800 number on the tube—while you were in the middle of pumping his uh, uh?"

"Penis. Pumping his penis. You can say it. Yes, I had to ask them what I was doing wrong," she said, as if this were the most normal course of action one would take during this process.

"So, what did they tell you, try two rubber bands and call me in the morning?"

"Oh, that's funny," she said throwing her head back and jutting out her chin, but most of all, she stopped talking.

"OK. I'm sorry, go ahead and finish the story." I wanted this saga over and didn't want to revisit it later.

"I wasn't doing anything wrong, his equipment is just shot. Kaput. Finished."

"His penis is out of warranty? Can you get a refund on the marriage license?" I asked with all the seriousness I could muster.

"I'm never telling you anything, ever again." Julia crossed her arms over her chest as if she could not be coerced into further discussion. This faux insult lasted a nano second. "But, the answer is no, I can't get a refund on the pump either. So, I am divorcing S.J. and he is going to pay for it since I've paid for everything else since we've been married."

I didn't want to mention S.J. filing for bankruptcy would perhaps affect how fast he was going to pay to get the divorce filed. "Julia, I'm going to say a prayer that you find a good man. St. Ann, St. Ann, please find Julia a man."

"Y'all Catholics have a saint for everything, don't you? Well, if you ask St. Ann to find me a man, make sure you ask her to find me a rich one, and make him tall and good looking." Julia was a Baptist and scoffed at many Catholic traditions.

"This isn't like an order you can place at a drive-through window. You have to have faith that your prayer will be answered. Do you still have that big, Black and Tan Coonhound your neighbor left you when she died?" I said to change the subject.

Julia and I were both animal lovers, but she

took in all sad dog stories. I only took in sad Schnauzer stories. Once, she stopped on the interstate in the pouring rain and coaxed a lab mix into her Mercedes. She had mud all over the leather seats, up to her ankles, ruining her very expensive four-inch pumps. It probably cost more to clean the car seats and replace the shoes than pay for the divorce with S.J. Julia had her principles! She would not take any pet to a shelter, and now she had another mouth to feed. This is how Julia and I, kindred spirits who loved animals, are friends in spite of many other things that we do not have in common.

Julia was dating S.J. when I first met her. We both were working at the phone company. S.J. told you, and would tell you often, he was a retired athlete. I'm not sure what he retired from as he never finished his story, or he changed the subject if you got around to asking. He stood 6'9" and carried an extra one hundred and fifty pounds. I felt petite standing next to both of them. S.J. drank a lot and he turned into a mean drunk. I can't imagine what possessed Julia to marry this buffoon, but marry him she did. S.J. might be what got Julia into taking on stray dogs, or maybe the dogs influenced Julia to take on S.J.

After her neighbor died in the hospital, Julia kept the 120 lb. Black and Tan Coonhound she was watching for her. S.J. started to rag on her about all the dogs she was taking care of. His drinking, saying negative things about the dogs, and his inability to sexually please Julia, bought him a one-way ticket out the front door.

"Yes, I still have the Coonhound. Why? Do you have a saint for him, too?"

"As a matter of fact, we do. Our dog saint is Saint Francis of the Animals. Before you ask, there is no cat saint so he has to do overtime for cats and all other animals."

"Wow. You Catholics gyp the animals out of their own saints when you have a saint for every other people thing, right? Isn't there Saint Lucy for the eyes, Saint Ann for a man, Saint Rapunzel for hair . . ."

"There is no Saint Rapunzel. That's a fairy tale. You are going to get us both struck by lightning. I'm going to get hit by being in close proximity to you. Now stop."

As I inched through the French Quarter, I tried not to hit drunken tourists. Men walked around looking up at women on the balconies lifting their shirts, or at women in the street pulling up their shirts all for a pair of beads. No one looked at traffic or oncoming cars.

The barkers all along Bourbon Street stood in doorways and tried to coerce tourists walking by to come in and enjoy the entertainment—for a price, of course. The price usually involved a two drink minimum. Two drinks in a Bourbon Street club costs you about the same as ten in a regular bar. Barkers opened the club doors long enough for anyone thinking about entering to get a glimpse of almost naked girls dancing on the bar. Then, you had to pony up the two drink minimum to go in and get a better look.

Club Bare Minimum didn't have a barker. Their doorman worked as the bouncer, and stood just inside the door out of sight. One of the very young and attractive girls stood in the doorway in her top hat, long gloves, tuxedo bow tie, G-string, and Pasties with a come hither look inviting men in. I couldn't figure out what men thought they could see by going inside the club when they already saw it all out here on the sidewalk.

Using the pretty girls over big hulky bouncers at the door was novel. The girls performed exotic dancing. Technically, they did not strip, meaning they didn't take it all off. They left on so little I didn't think it merited debate.

When I pulled up to the front door Julia jumped out and said, "Leave the keys. C'mon inside." A man, I did not see when I pulled up, stepped out, and Julia said to him, "Jim, park this in the VIP lot."

Jim, must have been standing inside the door behind the girl working the street. He looked to be about 6'3" tall and 200 pounds of solid muscle wearing the tightest shirt and jeans I have ever seen on anyone. Before I could argue with Julia, Jim opened my door and helped me out by the elbow while I held Isabella. He didn't look like the kind of guy you could reason with or have any sort of discussion with for that matter. His appearance and demeanor made me think Jim's actions were louder than his words.

I stood there on Bourbon Street in front of an exotic dancing club and watched my mother's station wagon be driven away by some guy named Jim to God knows where. Oh right, the VIP lot. I doubt I could find it, and it didn't matter since I didn't get a claim check.

"Julia, I'm only going to be here for a minute. Won't Jim wonder why he's parking my car and I have a dog?"

"Jim doesn't wonder. C'mon," she said halfway through the door. I hurried after her, or else I'd have to wait on the street alone—being gawked at by the drunken tourists. I managed to catch up to her when she said, "Follow me to my dressing room." Once in the dressing room she began to transform into the entertainer. She instructed me to call her by her stage name, Jewel, while we were in the club. The dressing room was the size of a broom closet. To pass someone you literally had to face each other, stepping sideways like crabs in order to squeeze by. Metal lockers the size of cereal boxes lined the wall. They were stacked seven high and five across. Julia found an empty locker and started to undress. She handed me her clothes and said, "Here, put these in one of those." There was no way all the clothes she wore into the club were going to fit in one of these lockers. She needed one just for her purse which was the size of a Mardi Gras float.

"This isn't going to work. All this stuff won't fit." I said.

"Look, there are several lockers empty. Put my stuff in the empty ones and look around in my purse. I have a couple of combo locks. Use them." Jewel said.

"What's going to happen when your manager sees me in here with Isabella?" I asked.

"If you knew half of what goes on in here, the dog won't faze him. Trust me." Julia kept changing out of her clothes and into her costume. It took her forever to get the smallest articles of the costume affixed to her person so as not to move or fall off. I didn't see how it mattered since there was nothing left to the imagination even with them in place.

Dancers and bartenders all wore the same costume, the bare minimum. Julia's costume was the same get-up as the girl at the door. Julia's started with a Tuxedo jacket over the pasties which she would remove before making her way into the exotic part of her performance, i.e. the pole.

The top hat covered more than the rest of the costume put together. You could put Julia's, I mean Jewel's, entire costume in the hat. All the dancers wore the same long gloves, tuxedo bow tie, G-string, pasties, and top hat, but added their own accessories to make them stand out as performers like tuxedo jackets, feather boas or giant fans.

Once I had most of her clothes stuffed into three compartments and locked, I asked her for directions to the ladies' room. She instructed me to leave the broom closet, umm, dressing room, go to the hallway and look for the first door on the right marked with an L for ladies. I left Julia holding Isabella until I came back.

The door to the ladies' room was narrower than the average width of standard doors. Everything in the French Quarter was built smaller. These structures are over 200 years old, and built for smaller people long before beignets and daiquiris added to the need for oversized doorways. People were shorter and smaller and had smaller feet, so steps were narrower with a lower rise and interior doorways didn't need to be very wide. I had to turn sideways to get through the door into the area with the toilet and sink. Once inside, I sat, grateful for a quiet moment alone. As I contemplated my next move I heard snoring. I stopped thinking about how to get back into

Charity when the snoring grew louder and added on a whistle chaser. I looked up and realized the sound came through the vent directly over my head as I sat on the commode. I gathered myself up as fast as I could, and ran to find Julia.

"Julia! There is someone hiding in the ceiling in the ladies' room looking through the vent when you squat!" I said in a frantic whisper.

"What?" Julia didn't stop putting on her makeup. "I told you to call me Jewel in here. There are always Peeping Toms in there."

"This guy is not peeping, he's snoring and he's in the ceiling."

"What do you mean in the ceiling?" She stopped applying eyeliner and looked at me.

"Come and see, or rather, come and hear." I said leading her to the ladies' room. At the door I put my finger to my lips to keep quiet so we wouldn't wake him up. We both couldn't fit so I pushed Jewel/Julia into the room with the toilet so she could be under the vent. I pointed to the vent above the toilet. We both heard it, a low exhale with a whistle sound followed by an inhaling stutter-snore. I was holding Isabella who cocked her head, the same as we did, trying to figure out what was up there.

We backed out of the bathroom and when we got in the hall Jewel said, "That dumb bunny. I bet he crawled up from the men's room side."

"I think you should call the police." I said, thinking this provided an opportune time to leave during the confusion. I wanted to get my car and continue on my mission even if I had to do it without her help.

She said, "You're right. Wait here." She ran off and returned with Pinky, the manager.

Pinky looked to be in his fifties, wore his hair in a neon pink-spiked mohawk and carried a cat-o-nine tails over the shoulder of his sleeveless leather vest, no shirt underneath. His six pack looked like it was working on being a keg. After a brief introduction as being Julia's friend and ride, he conducted an up and down visual review of me and then the situation in the ladies' room. He didn't ask about or act like he noticed Isabella.

"Don't let anyone go in there. I'm calling the cops," Pinky said as he marched off to find a phone. Over his shoulder he shouted, "Jewel, don't let her leave, she's a witness."

"Witness? No, no, no, no, no, no. I can't wait for the police." I tried to answer as he bolted off to make the call. It was going to take at least an hour for the police to get here, and another hour for them to figure out the situation, take notes, statements, and arrest this clown. It could take hours before I could return to Charity. If the police put my name on a complaint it was sure to find it's way into Dante's hands, and subsequently, my parents. This couldn't get any worse. But, I have been wrong before, and I would be wrong again.

"Julia, I mean, Jewel tell Pinky I have to leave," I said trying to appeal to her for help.

"No can do. Pinky's the man. What he says goes. The cops aren't gonna care if some Peeping Tom sees us. You're a patron, a tourist-type person. This is clearly a violation of your privacy. This is bad for Ceiling Boy. Sorry, you have to wait."

"I don't think someone snoring while I sit on the throne is a violation of my privacy. I didn't see him, I heard him. How much do you think he could see? He's asleep—and snoring. You . . . you and I heard him snoring. Maybe I am violating his nap time," I said.

"You can't get your car if Pinky tells Jimbo not to let you leave. This won't take long." Julia busied herself putting on more makeup, lots and lots of makeup. "Here, you want to try some?" she offered me her brushes.

"No, I have to leave, and I don't want to get arrested looking like a streetwalker if I ever get out of here."

Just then Suzanne squeezed into the dressing room to get ready for her shift. "What's with the ladies' room?" she asked. "Pinky said don't go in there. Where are we supposed to go?"

I explained what was going on and Suzanne wasn't even fazed. She said, "I'll go in the men's room if I have to. I grew up with brothers, what's the big deal? And what's with the dog? You rescue another one?"

"No, this dog belongs to the guy I kissed at the parade." I said.

Suzanne stopped changing clothes and faced me to give me her full attention. "Oh, this oughtta be good. Go on."

I told her what had happened, and that I wanted to get back into the hospital to tell Jiff his dog was okay.

"Why don't you just call and leave a message?" Suzanne asked.

"If I call and leave my name, it's possible whoever shot him might be able to figure out who has his dog and who I am."

"Good point. You know, I think you should consider getting your own place. You are up to your neck in personal stuff with your family, Dante, and his family, and they all have a ringside seat to everything you do. Wait til they hear all this," she said.

"My mother said if I move out—and no respectable woman moves out on her own without a husband—I can't come back if I don't make it."

"Well, thank God." said Julia, now completely transformed into Jewel. "For a minute I thought you might have to suck it up and crawl back to Mommy Dearest if you needed to. Knowing you can't move back means you have to make it. The ol' ball and chain is doing you a favor!"

"Your mother's trying to control you. Besides, your dad would help you. He might even move out with you," Suzanne laughed at her own joke. "Listen, my roommate is leaving to get her own place. You can move in with me. Heck, I don't care how many dogs you bring home."

"You're right. I have to get through this with Jiff and Isabella and review my expenses. I'll let you know in a couple of days. Thanks." I said.

The waiting began. The police arrived an hour later even though their precinct is one block away. They questioned me and continued to the ladies' room where they demanded, using a megaphone, for the guy to come out. After a few shouts at him, he woke up, and you could hear him mutter in a groggy voice, "Man, I'm stuck."

The police turned to Pinky, 'Jewel', and me who were standing there waiting for the conclusion and said, "This is a matter for the Fire Department. If he's stuck, they get people out, not the police. After they get him out, call us back and we'll arrest him."

"Officer, I can leave, right?" I asked, oh so nicely.

"No. you need to be here when we get back to

press charges." said the officer.

"I don't even know what I am pressing charges for." I said.

"Indecent exposure," said Jewel.

"Mine or yours? I was on the toilet when I heard him snoring. What do you think he saw?"

"Criminal mischief," said Pinky.

"If it is mischief, then how is it criminal?" I asked, frustrated that no one saw the folly in any of it.

"Your civil rights have been violated," offered Jewel.

"No. I think that's a stretch." I just looked at her.

"Can't you wait 'til the Fire Department gets him out?" I pleaded with the officer.

"No, we have other calls. Just call in and say you got the guy out of the ceiling. Dispatch will send us right back here." said Officer Not-So-Helpful.

What? Now, we had to call the Fire Department, and no telling how long it will take for them to get here on a parade night. Julia put her foot over the back of a chair and started stretching getting ready for her performance. The police officer almost walked into the wall. Pinky went to call the Fire Department, but before he did, he directed me to stay in front of the ladies' room and tell the women patrons it was out of order. To the few who did need the facilities I had to recommend they go elsewhere as a man was stuck in the ceiling over the toilet. One woman didn't care and pushed past me to get in. I guess her bathroom philosophy is, "Any port in a storm."

When I redirected women to go elsewhere, they went to get their dates and left the club. When Pinky saw he was losing patrons, he went to Plan B. He stationed me in front of the ladies' room door with the dog in my lap and wanted me to direct the women to the men's room. Pinky would chase the guys out and hold the door while the women used it. While I sat with Isabella guarding the bathroom, I must have nodded off for a few minutes. A voice boomed in my ear and almost levitated me out of my chair. It was a fireman saying, "Miss, wake up. We need to get in there."

The Fire Department had arrived—two hours after the police left, and they are located in the French Quarter, two blocks away from the club. Pinky told them it was not life or death. I started thinking it could become Pinky's death if I had to wait here much longer. They took what felt like another hour running from the ladies' room to the mens' room assessing the situation. They concluded they could not pull or push this guy through the opening at either end. They decided they had to cut him out of the ceiling. This required many more trips back and forth to the truck.

Now, the entire bar was overrun by firemen preparing for the big rescue. The performances stopped along with the drinking and paying customers. Pinky was not happy. All the dancers in their costumes, or lack thereof, created distractions for the firemen. It seemed they had to make many more trips than necessary past the girls to get all the equipment needed from their truck. They were always forgetting something. They trekked in and out bringing in saws, the jaws of life, and various other equipment that looked like it could dismantle a New York City skyscraper.

The fire chief arrived, and before any work could be performed, he discussed with Pinky whether the Historical Society should be consulted since this had to do with defacing one of the French Quarter's original sites. Who were they kidding? This was a titty bar, and Pinky said so. After this useless discussion of its historical significance they decided if the guy remained in the ceiling much longer it might be detrimental to his life expectancy. They finally started cutting.

Once the firemen cut a slice in the ceiling plaster, the trapped man's weight caused the rest of the ceiling to give way and he crashed to the floor, smacked his head on the porcelain toilet bowl and was knocked unconscious. He started bleeding everywhere.

The firemen started picking up their equipment and leaving.

"Wait." I said, "You need to take him to the hospital. Look, he's hurt."

"We only rescue and are not tasked with administering first aid or transporting to a care facility. We can't take him anywhere. You have to call EMS." said the fire chief.

"But y'all are the reason he hit his head."

"No," the chief corrected me, "he's the reason he hit his head. We're outta here. If someone else gets stuck or something catches fire, call us." And with that they recovered their gear and disappeared.

I couldn't believe it. What if EMS got there and he died, would we need to call and wait for the coroner? Maybe by then, they wouldn't need me as the complaining witness.

I followed Pinky to his office where he dialed 911 to the Emergency Medical Service. I have to admit, Pinky scared me, but the fear of being stuck there the whole night scared me more. I couldn't take it any longer. When he got off the phone, I said, "Pinky, this is going to take hours for the EMS guys to get here, take him to an emergency room, then wait for the police to take my statement and arrest him. I am happy to come back to do this, but I need to get to Charity. A friend of mine got shot at the parade tonight. I need to get to the hospital and see how he's doing."

"You're taking the dog with you, right?"

Jewel walked up complaining, "This is the biggest cluster I've ever seen." The Peeping Tom ran off business which negatively affected her tips. "Pinky, can I leave? I am not making any money tonight, and none of us can use the ladies' room. She's my ride."

"Can you send Jim to get my car so we can go?" I asked.

He waved us off saying "Yes, and take Suzanne with you. Jimbo, go get her car!" he yelled.

As we pulled away from the curb, the EMS truck screamed up Bourbon Street and pulled right into our space. I wondered how many trips these guys would have to make to their crash truck to get Peeping Tom on his way to Charity.

"God! How do y'all work in there? I felt like I was stuck in a bad disco movie," I said to Suzanne as we drove off.

"Yeah, it looks like the 80's took a dump in there," she answered.

Chapter Eight

"WE NEED A plan. We need help, and I think I know who might be willing to give it to us," I said to Julia.

"Whose gonna help? Huh? This is on us, and by us, I mean you." Julia said.

"I was thinking of Stan."

"Oh yeah, Stan will help you." said Suzanne. "Old Stan, the Duck Man."

"That guy you grew up with, that Stan? The one who dresses up like a duck?" Julia's face was all screwed up and she looked at me like I had grown feathers. She had heard all about Stan from Suzanne and I over lunch one day.

Stan lived to right wrongs and help those in need. He could hardly be considered a crime fighter. He was more of a prank fighter. During high school days he took on the persona of Duck Man, and it bode well for Stan since most pranksters in our schools didn't carry automatic weapons. He made himself a Duck Man costume with an orange duckbilled cap, a white mask and a red cape. He wore a white button down shirt and white jeans to finish his disguise. His footwear of choice were his running shoes. He took an old baseball bat and cut it down to the grip. He cut out a web foot from an old inner tube tire and glued it to the end. The foot became known as his *assistant* in case he had to duck-slap someone about to kick his ass. He named his assistant, The Quacker.

"Stan is a nice guy and he'll be happy to help an old friend. He'll be up, he works late hours at home. Drop me home. I can't be a witness to any more of this tonight. My head is going to explode and I have a class tomorrow," Suzanne said from the back seat.

"How do you know Stan will be up?" I asked.

"He's working on a patent for me on that streaming roach spray can I designed. I sometimes call him when I get off work which is usually late, and he always answers. He never sounds like I just woke him up. He's a bit of a night owl and a workaholic," Suzanne replied in a very tired voice. "He will be thrilled to see you, Brandy."

"Julia, you'll love Stan. He sews." By now she had morphed out of the entertaining Jewel.

"What? Is he gay?" she asked.

"Let me tell her," Suzanne offered. "You are not going to tell it right. When he decided to be Duck Man he thought he needed a disguise. One day he brought home fabric and was sewing a cape and mask on his mother's sewing machine. When she saw him she asked, 'Stan, are you gay?' I guess since Stan was in high school and didn't have a steady girlfriend, his mother got worried when she saw him sewing clothes. No, he isn't gay. He's just a nice guy and very creative." Suzanne finished the story laughing.

"Okay, maybe not gay, maybe he's just a momma's boy," Julia said unimpressed.

"He's performed many humanitarian efforts," I replied. My feelings were hurt for Stan.

Stan rode around on his motorcycle in the Duck Man outfit stopping minor crimes like purse snatching or helping old people cross streets. There were some punks in the neighborhood who drove by the projects in cars and water ballooned the old black people sitting on their porches. Stan attempted to reason with this gang to no avail, hence he needed the assistance of The Quacker. After the gang refused to stop water ballooning, Stan decided he had to do something. He borrowed metal garbage can lids and gave them to the old people to act as shields when the water ballooners rode by. This might have been the only time he had to duck slap someone. The punks were some kind of ticked off at Stan for putting the kibosh on their fun. When they tried to jump Stan, the assistant came to the rescue and fended off the attack.

I remembered the dog story and figured this would make Julia see Stan in a better light. "He won my eternal devotion when he stopped a man kicking a dog. Stan jumped off his motorcycle and kicked the guy in his butt. When the guy turned around, Stan decked him, and brought me the dog." Julia listened but didn't jump on board and join the Stan Fan Club.

Stan, Suzanne and I grew up on the same block. Stan went to Jesuit, an all boys Catholic School and Suzanne and I went to an all girls Catholic School about one bus stop away. We rode the bus in the morning together and stayed friends.

Suzanne and I thought Stan would go into a crime fighting career like law enforcement or as a DEA agent. He chose law school following in the steps of his dad, a successful attorney. Duck Man's Daddy settled a very big tobacco suit earning his firm millions and then moved the family to the Lakefront into a very big, very nice house. Stan's early antics did put him in touch with juvenile delinquents and subsequent career criminals that he now defended or sometimes prosecuted. Stan figured he could do more good with a law degree than the Duck Man costume. Before he hung it up he invited me to ride along with him on his last caper. I felt like a Bond girl. Stan and Dante were friends, and Stan, being the honorable Duck Man, would never ask me out knowing Dante liked me. I hoped Stan still carried the torch enough to help me.

"Stan just popped into my head," Suzanne said. "Maybe because I'm delirious from lack of food and sleep."

"The Duck? You want to ask a man who dresses up like a duck to help you? He would have his tail feathers handed to him, if not by the guys out to get Heinkel, then Dante. Forget about him."

"Can you please just drop me at a bus stop. I can't take any more of this." Suzanne said from the back seat.

"I'm taking you home, relax. Julia and I will go to Stan's." I told Suzanne. Then to Julia, I continued, "We-e-e-e-ell, technically, he has not been the Duck since high school. I'm out of ideas, and if you don't have a better one, then I'm asking him." With that we dropped Suzanne in front of her apartment. She jumped out of the car before it stopped. I took a good look at her location. I liked it and I could see myself living there. There was a large fenced yard for the dogs. It could work. I told her I wanted to move in, but still had to check the finances to make sure I could. We waited until Suzanne opened her front door, went inside and waved goodnight to us, signaling all looked safe, before we drove away.

I drove to Stan's home on the Lakefront, in the

same high rent section of the parish where the Lakefront Towers are located.

I rang the bell and smiled, glad Julia talked me into wearing the scoop neck sweater. I took a very deep breath hoping to accentuate my positive attributes. The porch light came on and a very surprised, but smiling Stan stood in the doorway holding an old-fashioned glass of scotch. He was dressed in purple sweat pants with GEAUX TIGERS down one leg and a matching sweat shirt with LSU in giant gold letters across his chest.

"Hello Brandy, fancy you calling on me in the middle of the night." Stan said smiling and stepping aside to invite us in. He paid so much attention to me he almost shut the door on Julia. She hated Stan instantly.

"I'm sorry, I know this is late, and I hope we aren't disturbing you." When I saw the drink in his hand I added, "Oh, my gosh, I hope you don't have company. I really need your help. I just dropped Suzanne off at her house and she said you might be awake."

"Do you turn into a frog or maybe a duck after midnight?" Julia asked. I don't think he heard her or maybe he ignored her.

Stan answered, "I was up working on a case and just poured myself a Scotch by way of winding down. It's a nice surprise seeing you, Brandy, no matter what time it is." He acted like he hadn't noticed Julia at all.

"Stan, this is my friend Julia."

Stan extended his hand to shake Julia's and asked, "So where did you go to high school?"

"What is it with y'all and high school? Didn't any of you go to college?" Julia turned to me leaving Stan's extended hand waiting for a handshake.

Before she could do any more social damage and provoke Stan into throwing us out of his home, I launched into my dilemma. I recounted the shooting, rescuing Isabella while fleeing for our lives, and tried to avoid mentioning Dante through it all. I needed access back into the hospital. Stan took it all in with his eyes trying to observe my rather low neckline without looking right at my chest. Then he said, apologetically, he was not willing to don the Duck Man persona anymore.

"Well, why not?" I whined. "Why won't you help me?" I hated it when I sounded like this.

"I didn't say I wouldn't help you, I just can't be Duck Man. If I get caught wearing that outfit, I'll never be taken seriously in court again, and my Dad would oust me from the firm. One of you can be Duck Man. You are both tall and could pull off being a guy. Besides who, in this city, during Mardi Gras, is going to challenge you wearing a costume?"

He had a point.

"Also, you need to ride my motorcycle. It's the vehicle of choice for Duck Man, so Brandy that means you. I know you can drive a motorcycle. I taught you how when I lived across the street from you, remember?"

Stan was more than willing to teach me how to drive a motorcycle. His dad bought him one as soon as he was old enough to drive. He used to sit behind me and put his arms around me. Stan, Dante and I learned to drive on Stan's first motorcycle and spent all summer on it. I continued driving and riding them with Dante and his brothers after Stan moved. They all had one at some time or another and I always tagged along, taking turns driving them while the other rode on the back. Sometimes Stan would buzz by my high school and give me a ride home on the back of his bike.

"OK." I said, "will you take care of Isabella for us while we go back to Charity to see what we can find out and tell Heinkel his dog is OK?" I asked.

Julia was aghast at the idea of us wearing the Duck Man costume and both of us dressing like men.

"You have lost your mind. I'm not riding on the back of a motorcycle with you and I'm not wearing that nutty costume. People will think we are related to that kook, Ruthie, the Duck Girl in the French Quarter. You know the one. She feeds the ducks that live with her and follow her around. Are you sure he isn't related to Ruthie?" Julia asked questions out loud about people as if they weren't standing right there next to us. She needed to work on her people skills.

Ruthie was a street person. Everyone knew Ruthie and the residents of the French Quarter loved her and fed her and her ducks. She was an eccentric local that was harmless and everyone watched out for her.

Stan knew how to roll with it. He looked at Julia and asked, "Did you say you know each other from charm school?"

"I'll wear the Duck Man costume," I said answering Julia. "You'll drive the station wagon in case we are separated from each other. Besides, if anyone sees us in the station wagon they will know who we are. If you are with Duck Man and you're not wearing a costume, someone, like those two goons, might figure out who we are."

"Exactly." Stan said while leading us through his home and to the costume closet. The costume closet was bigger than any room in our house. It was a huge walk in with double hung sides that went on for miles. One half of the space was dedicated to womens' costumes and the other half to mens'. There seemed to be hundreds of them. Stan had a bigger inventory than the costume shop on Magazine. Julia's face lit up when she found the French Maid and Dallas Cowgirl cheerleader costumes. The look on her face showed a new appreciation and a hint of interest in Stan.

"I think I should wear one of these. Stan, you ole dog, this is a very interesting side of you." Julia held the outfits in front of her trying to decide which one to wear. On the men's side of the closet I looked at the Village People collection and tried to envision Stan in the construction hat, no shirt and tool belt. The construction worker is my personal fantasy. He had all kinds of costumes from Super Heroes like Spiderman and Superman, to animals, Halloween costumes and even a Santa suit. I could almost hear Julia thinking, Stan is either kinky or goes to a lot of parties.

"You into role play, Stan?" Julia asked with her eyebrow arched.

We grew up in a Superhero world. Cartoons, movies and TV teach us that men who are superheroes are the successful ones, the desirable ones. These caricatures create an unreasonable expectation on men as to what women expect from them. Maybe Stan felt the need to be souped-up to attract women.

"Julia, I think you should wear this one." Stan showed her a white gorilla costume that completely covered the head, hands and feet.

"Are you some kinda fairy?" Julia asked. When

she pronounced fairy in her Baton Rouge twang it sounded like furry. Stan looked confused.

"Julia, that looks hot," I could hardly contain myself from laughing. I said it before the two of them could fight over it.

"You both are a riot. Yes, it's looks hot, as in Africa hot," she fired back. "Now why would I wear that? That's not something I'd be caught dead in."

"I had that custom made for the Zoo To Do the year the Audubon Society got a white gorilla. It's a very well made costume." Stan said defending it by pointing out its finer features.

"Look this covers your head and no one will know who you are. You can wear flats and look almost a foot shorter. This is about stealth and covertness. This isn't the time to be sexy and draw attention to either of us." I said.

"If I have to wear a costume, I'll decide which one." Julia's adamant stance indicated I needed leverage. I needed to pull out the big gun, my ace in the hole.

"You are forcing me to come clean on your last escapade with Dante's brother, Daniel." I added, "I'll tell my mother, Dante, and Daniel's mother."

Drawing in a huge breath she almost exploded with "You promised! You even pinky swore that you would keep that a secret. Now, even the Duck here knows."

"Stan doesn't know . . . yet. But I'll be forced to tell him every juicy tidbit." I added emphasis to juicy and tidbit in case she missed the point. You can't overstate the obvious with Julia.

"Whatever you tell me is considered attorney client privilege if anyone would ever ask me. As it is, I'll come bail you two out if you get arrested in these outfits. I can get you to sign a retainer that I'm your attorney, representing you, if that makes you more comfortable telling me." Stan tried the back door approach by way of getting the Daniel information out of me. Julia was not having any of it.

"Don't tell him another thing. Give me that damn gorilla suit. We had a deal," Julia looked deflated and Stan looked disappointed.

Stan had his arms crossed and then put one hand on his chin with the other hand on his elbow. It was his thinking pose. He started to instruct me in Duck Man habits and actions to take. He still had the entire outfit including the running shoes. He made me put it all on. The shoes were too big and I couldn't walk in them.

"I think I have a pair of shoes in the car. My mother's Jazzercise bag is in there and she wears my old tennis shoes." I went out to the wagon and found them. Stan's boxy shirt and jeans made me look more like a guy.

"If you get in a jam, or get arrested, call me

and I can get you out. If I'm Duck Man, then I'll be in jail sitting next to you. I have my career to think of. You just walk in like you own the place. Try not to draw any attention to yourself."

"She is wearing a Duck suit riding a motorcycle following a white gorilla driving a green station wagon, and you don't think she will draw attention to herself? The gorilla will be driving the getaway car? Do I have this right?" We both ignored Julia's sarcasm.

Stan continued with his instruction. He was positively exuberant to see his alter ego back in action. "Do not use the Duck Foot unless you think you are in real danger. You can really hurt someone with it. Use it in self defense if someone looks like they are going to hurt you. No one is going to think much of you in a costume. This is New Orleans. You just walk in like normal, do what you need to do, and leave. Remember, walk with a purpose."

"Instead of waddling with a purpose?" Julia was still at it and had not warmed up to the idea of the gorilla suit or the mission.

"I always hoped I would find someone to carry on the Duck Man tradition. I'm glad it's you, Brandy." Stan said beaming.

"I am getting misty-eyed." Julia said dabbing at her invisible tears. "In case you haven't noticed, Stan, Duck Man is you, and you are a man.

Brandy has boobs."

Undaunted, he added, "Well, that will add to Duck Man's mystique. Harder to figure out who Duck Man is if everyone's looking for a man. Besides there are more cross dressers here than anywhere on the planet. No one will think anything of it." Stan glowed over the idea of Duck Man's revival. He rummaged around in the bottom of the closet coming out with a roll of duct tape.

"Here, just tape your chest with this and you won't look so, so" he paused, then added "girly."

"Duct tape? Really?" asked Julia.

I didn't have the heart to tell him I had no intention of accepting the Quacker and taking on the Duck Man tradition, but I needed a diversion to get into the hospital past the cops, and this seemed like the best option on short notice.

Stan went about finding all the feet and hands to the gorilla suit. He gave Julia a pair of flip flops and told her she had to take off the high heels since the gorilla feet were designed to slip over flat shoes. She grabbed them and began putting on the costume with unsportsmanlike conduct.

Stan gave us two walkie talkies with a good range so we could stay in contact. He instructed us how to use them. He stood back to review his work and our outfits. The gorilla suit looked the same on Julia as it did on the hanger. She didn't fill it out so she made a tall, skinny ape. "Well, you look about as ready as you're going to get," he said.

"Is that your idea of a pep talk?" Julia asked. "Cuz, if it is, don't ever think about volunteering to answer the Suicide Hot Line."

"O.K. I feel ready," I said trying to keep those two from going at each other. This began to feel like one of those ideas that was great before you started actually doing it. It was go time. Stan handed me the keys to the motorcycle and I handed Julia the keys to the station wagon and we were off. Her bra was still holding up the fender.

Chapter Nine

THE PLAN SEEMED simple enough. We were going to walk in through the emergency entrance, Julia going in first as the gorilla to divert attention. She would alert me on the two way radio if a problem arose. I would follow about half a corridor back and she would instruct me over the walkie talkie if she spotted Dante so I could avoid him and get in to see Heinkel. I didn't want to be herded off and sent home by Dante for the third time in twenty-four hours. If he saw me again, he might arrest me in order to keep me in one place for the rest of the night.

If I didn't return in thirty minutes Julia was to drive my mother's station wagon back to Stan's. If it took me too long to get in and see Heinkel, then I would ride back to Stan's on the motorcycle. I didn't feel good about Julia going first. Her big gorilla heart just didn't seem into it. It was now going on three A.M., the hospital seemed more awake and active in the middle of the night than it was in the middle of the day. The staff cleaned floors, restocked cabinets and nurses pushed pill carts from room to room up and down the halls checking on patients.

We passed an ER and a woman dressed like a French Maid with a stethoscope and ID badge around her neck pulled Julia into the room saying "Our party is in here, you animal." Oh boy, I will have hell to pay over this. Julia disappeared behind doors marked ER 4. As the doors closed I caught a glimpse of the hospital costume party in full swing for those who had worked the 3-11 shift. The bad news: I lost Julia as a lookout. The good news: There were lots of the hospital staff in costumes. That would help me get past any policemen.

Any policemen, except the two at Jiff Heinkel's door. These two New Orleans Police Department officers, dressed in SWAT team uniforms, were stationed there and would not let anyone in.

I approached them and said in the deepest voice I could muster, "I have information for Mr. Heinkel, I need to get it to him." I wished Julia was here in that French Maid costume. My chances would have been better.

"Give me some ID and you can go in," one of the cops said to me. The second guy didn't speak to me but gave me a brief look up and down, then went back to staring at the opposite wall. I felt my pockets while I looked back to the nurses' station acting as if I left it there.

"I left it downstairs in my locker, after I got dressed in this crazy costume," I tried and waited to see if that would get me a pass. After a couple of awkward moments neither one spoke so I asked, "Can you give him this message for me?" Not giving either one an opportunity to say no, I continued, "A lady called and said he asked her to check on Isabella. It's his dog. She said Isabella is all right and will keep the dog for him."

"And, you are?" asked the one not starting at the wall and writing it all down in his notepad.

"I'm the nurse who worked the emergency room when Mr. Heinkel came in. I took the message from the lady about his dog. She didn't leave her name. She just said she's the friend Mr. Heinkel asked to take care of his dog."

He told me to wait there. He went into the room while the other one stopped looking at the wall and started staring at me. I smiled. I heard him telling Jiff that some guy brought a message for him about Isabella being safe. Great, he thought I was a guy. Stan would be so proud. If this cop knew I was a girl dressed like a guy to look like a duck he might haul me off to the psycho ward.

When he returned, I thanked them and left to go back to the ER. I needed to find Julia and get out of here fast. I rounded a corner out of sight from the two cops and saw a phone at an unattended nurses' station. The temptation was too great so I dialed Jiff's room number and he answered. I told him I was the person he asked to help Isabella. I was the one who just sent the message in with the SWAT commando stationed outside his room.

He thanked me. I didn't want to hang up, and after a long silent moment he asked me, "Are you the girl I kissed?"

Unprepared for the question, I stuttered, "Uh yeah. Yes. Yes, I am."

"I know your name is Brandy and I know you rescue Schnauzers cuz I'm on a first name basis with Einstein. Look, I'm getting out of here tomorrow around noon. The bullet only grazed my arm. It really hurts but the doctor said I was lucky. They want to keep me tonight for observation."

"Oh, that's good. I, I, I," I couldn't think of what else to say.

"I know I have asked you a lot already and you don't even know me, but would you come pick me up tomorrow? I seem to be without transportation other than a wheelchair, and the hospital will only lend me that to the door."

Silence. More silence. I tried to figure out a way to tell him about the thugs at his apartment, when he said,

"Are you still there?"

"I'm still here. I'd be happy to pick you up. That way I can bring Isabella back to you." How stupid did that sound. I was not getting into this hospital with his dog.

"Well, good, thanks. I'll see you tomorrow. My doctor said I could leave anytime after lunch."

"At one o'clock tomorrow then. I'll park and come in to get you."

"You might have to wheel me out. They don't let anyone walk out. You have to be rolled out in a wheelchair, and then they dump you out of it when you get to the door. Don't worry, you won't have to carry me because I can walk." I pictured him smiling when he said that.

"No problem, I think I can handle a wheelchair. See you tomorrow." I hung up and boogied off that floor before a real nurse asked for my credentials.

I went back to ER 4 and found Julia alone at the party. She still had on the costume and when I grabbed her arm, she reeled around as if to yell at me but only said, "Oh, it's you. Every woman in here has asked me to pick her up like King Kong so a friend can take her picture. Not one man has come over to talk to me."

"I guess the law of the jungle is apes rule." I said trying to cheer her up.

"I keep pointing to my back like it is the reason I can't pick them up. Talk about feeling invisible to men! This ape costume neutered me. I feel like one of your rescues. I was afraid to take off the head to get something to eat or drink, because someone might think I'm a pervert. Get me outta here. I'm sweating in this thing like a whore on dollar night," Julia said.

"That's such a nice thing to say. I'll have that visual in my head forever," and added, "But thank you, I couldn't have done this alone."

"I know you couldn't have and, you are not welcome. You owe me, and I plan to collect, when I'm ready."

As we exited the ER party, Joe, Dante's partner walked right past us. He didn't recognize either of us in the costumes. We walked out with a purpose.

On our way down the ramp at the Emergency Room exit we saw my mother's station wagon being driven away. We ran to the empty parking space watching the taillights disappear up Napoleon Avenue when Stan jumped out from behind some bushes scaring the hell out of us. Excited and shocked, we all talked at once.

"What are you doing here?" from both Julia and me in a chorus.

"I saw those guys turn on their headlights when you left my house and pull out after you. I thought you could use some backup."

"Why didn't you stop them from stealing the car?" I asked.

"Lotta help you are." Julia added.

"Did you see how huge those guys were?" he asked in self defense. "They got out of a squad car that stopped right up the street. It looks like the police knows them."

"Where did the cop who dropped them off go?" I asked Stan as a knot formed in my stomach.

"He parked after they got out and walked in the ER entrance right before you two walked out."

"Oh, God, that's Joe, Dante's partner." I said as the color felt like it left my face. "He knows who they are. Those are the guys that tried to break into Heinkel's apartment at the Towers."

"Well, that's not good." Stan said. "Dante's partner might be involved in getting Heinkel shot."

Stan grabbed my arms as my knees gave out under me. He sat me down on the curb.

"What will I tell Dante? What's my reason for seeing Joe drop those guys off at Charity. He's gonna kill me, or those two guys are gonna kill me, or my mother is gonna kill me for letting her car get stolen." I said.

Stan added, "The real question is what does Joe have to do with this?"

Julia added, "Look how popular you are now with so many people trying to kill you." If she was trying to make me feel better it didn't work. She took a step back after I gave her the look I inherited from my mother when she is displeased. When she felt a comfortable distance to blunder on, she added, "I think the brassiere holding up the bumper was like waving a red flag in front of those two neanderthals. They look cornfed, beefy, and dumb as rocks. I'm surprised they had the combined brain power to find the only avocado green station wagon in the city of New Orleans. Look on the bright side, you might not have to explain to your mother why her bumper is now a D cup."

"Julia, you're not helping." The developing situation and my lack of sleep made me crabby. "Stan, I still have the keys." I pulled out the car keys from Stan's jeans I was wearing. "How did they get the car started?"

"Hot wired, I'm sure. Guys like that can get in and start a car in seconds. Oh God! Now they know where you live from the registration in the car. We have to call the police to fill out the stolen car report." Stan was trying to calm me down and take charge but his voice was shaking worse than my knees.

"The police dropped them off at her mother's car, remember?" Julia answered Stan. "Maybe, you should try getting it back from those two guys instead of calling the police." Payback for the gorilla outfit was going to be endless.

At least we had left our purses and Julia's valuables at Stan's house. We had our IDs, keys and a few dollars and stuffed them in our bras and pockets in case we needed them. They knew where I lived, but I still had the house keys.

"You two girls take the truck. I'll take the motorcycle home. Meet me at my house. I'll work on finding the station wagon and getting a report filed." said Stan.

It was late and a good thing it was a Friday night so I didn't have to go to work the next day. Julia didn't have to go back to work until Saturday night. She jumped behind the wheel of the truck, pushed the seat all the way back as far as it would go and wiggled out of the gorilla suit. "I can't take another second in this thing. Think a Daiquiri will calm our nerves?" Without waiting for an answer she headed to the 24/7 drive thru Daiquiri Shoppe. She drove while I was lost in thought about the station wagon we had for so many years. I remembered the night that my mother took me to my first boy-girl King Cake party in the green machine. The memory, like the damp night air sent a shiver down my back when I thought about how it all went haywire like tonight.

The King Cake Party is the New Orleans introduction to the social scene for young people coming of dating age. Every adolescent in New Orleans waits for the invitation to a Mardi Gras King Cake party, your first boy-girl party where your parents have to decide whether to let you attend. These parties are the prelude to dating.

The King Cake is a large doughnut-shaped coffee cake, sprinkled with purple, green, and gold sugar with a plastic doll hidden inside. At these parties, the cake is sliced, everyone gets a piece and whoever gets the hidden doll in his or her piece, must give the next party. Parties are expected to happen weekly for the entire Mardi Gras season. This is only about six weeks. This creates great saga and drama in young lives and decidedly separates the popular from the unpopular.

The person who gets the piece that has the hidden doll is the night's "king" or "queen." That person with the doll then selects his or her reigning opposite. This makes for lifelong grudges if someone names a king that her friend likes. It is the first place you dance with boys and learn what morons they can be. These cakes make their debut every year on Twelfth Night, the official start of Mardi Gras, and are consumed in mass quantities until Lent.

So, with great enthusiasm and apprehension at thirteen, I was going to my first King Cake Party. My mother drove me and three of my friends in the family green station wagon. A girl from my class named Joyce had the first kick-off party at her parents' home.

Tonight, my big debut at a girl-boy party, and

I arrived in the family avocado green station wagon with my mother at the wheel. The boys in the hood all referred to it as the leaping lizard.

We found the house on the third pass when my mother slowed down to 50 mph so someone could catch a house number. She decided from inside the car, sitting behind the wheel the house didn't look like an opium den or brothel. She made a snap decision, slammed on the brakes, screeched to a stop. My friends and I got out of the station wagon. As we disembarked the green machine she said to me, "I will be back at eleven to pick you up. Oh, and Brandy, if you get the doll, swallow it. I'm not having a party with all these kids at our house." As I slammed the car door, she hit the gas and took the corner on two wheels heading home.

The party was uneventful, meaning, I did not get the piece of cake with the doll in it. So, I didn't need to try to swallow it or act like I didn't get it. I really had no idea how to pull that off and the thought of trying scared me to death.

The lights were very dim for dancing, something new to us, and we could barely see a thing. Two new guys we never saw before, walked in and the cute one walked straight over toward me. I was glad the music was so loud because I am sure I gasped as I grabbed Suzanne's hand. She followed my gaze, and was squeezing my hand in return. He came up and stood next to me smiling.

He put his hand out to take mine to slow dance. His friend asked Suzanne to dance. He said in my ear his name was Rick and we danced almost every song. He talked to me asking my name, school, where I lived, everything. He said he had his driver's license. We just kept dancing. Others at the party trickled out on the dance floor. Even when the music changed, we kept dancing slow, and talking. I started to wish this party would never end. Finally, I was having fun. He offered to give me a ride home. I thought, Wow, he must be sixteen years old! Then, BAM, it hit me. At eleven P.M. my mother was coming to pick us up. All of us. My mother would never approve of leaving a party, in a car with someone she didn't know.

I told him I had a ride with my friends. He offered to take my friends home as well. I did the only thing I could do. I lied.

I said I couldn't get in touch with my ride, and she was going to pick us up at a designated time. My dreamboat offered to take me home and let the ride take my friends. What planet did he beam down from? My new suitor asked for my phone number, and I gave it to him. Did I stop thinking altogether?

My mother showed up early, waited at the curb impatiently, honking the horn.

I said I had to go. He said he had a great time with me, and that he liked me. He liked me! For the first time in my life, I was *in like*! I felt like a helium balloon that needed to be tethered. I drifted out to the car. I'm sure we looked like little aliens getting into a big green space ship.

I got in the back seat and moved over, but not fast enough. While distracted by being *in like* my mother took off as Suzanne stepped off the ground and before the car door closed. With my mother behind the wheel everything had to happen fast. She had to make good time. It didn't matter where we were going or when we had to get there. We had to get to wherever we were going, and we could not waste any time doing it. It didn't matter that it was eleven P.M. on a Friday night with no school the next day. It didn't matter that we were thirteen years old, in the car with a parent driving us home for the night.

I didn't see the next thing coming. The cute guy, Rick, didn't tell me he was going to follow me home.

My mother left the neighborhood on two wheels, sped onto the highway slamming on the brakes at every stop light. She hit the gas and took off when the light changed to green like she got the flag at the Indy 500. She slammed to a stop at a red light when Rick and Eddie pulled up next to us driving his family wood paneled station wagon.

I thought we had something in common and took it as a good sign, until . . .

My mother blurts out, "Everyone lock your doors!"

He waved at us, so I waved back. My mother screamed, "What are you doing with your boy-crazy self?"

I tried to tell her I knew them. "Ma, you see, I," my answer cut short by the station wagon lunging forward causing my head to whiplash.

She stomped the gas pedal and took off at the green light, and Rick followed by moving into the lane behind us. At this point she started yelling at an even higher pitch. "See what you have gotten us into? Just shut up."

Since this was not the first, or the most unusual behavior my friends witnessed my mother doing, I knew better than to try and explain. They kept quiet hoping to arrive home alive. Despite several attempts I made trying to explain that I knew these boys, she continued to scream, "Just Shut Up! You and your boy-crazy self are going to get us all killed! You have us in enough trouble already!"

Did I hear right? She thought these guys were dangerous? She would soon realize that, not only was I boy crazy, but I fraternized with the two sociopaths at the party.

My friend, Suzanne looked at me with the "you know it is no use" eye roll. She has been my friend since second grade and knows the caffeine highs my mother can ride.

I tried to calm her before she pitched a full blown conniption fit. She screamed back at me cutting me off, "Don't Mom me, just shut up! Look at the mess you got us in."

My mother had it on some greater authority that Rick's family car was the vehicle of choice for the suburban hoodlum. I got a glimpse of the speedometer and she was doing 100 m.p.h. She began running red lights.

"I think I can lose these two." She said checking in the rear view mirror as she increased the distance between us, only because Rick respected traffic lights waiting for them to turn green. There were no other cars out, only us in the station wagon and the boys in the Woody. It was unbelievable, but Rick and his friend Eddie kept up with us. She got angrier by the minute making her drive faster and more reckless.

Riding shotgun, was my sister. Sherry wore her Snow White and the Seven Dwarfs' nightgown. She is two years younger than I, and an emotional diva. She could have been the eighth dwarf, Whiney. By age five she could increase the saga and drama when the order of events did not suit her by turning on the waterworks. Sherry had crying down to an art form and could dispense a flood of tears at a moment's notice. She wanted to go to the party. My parents allowed me to go and said she had to wait another year. Once the car chase started she saw her opportunity to add to my misery.

The boys were still close when my mother decided to peel off into Suzanne's quiet little neighborhood at eleven-fifteen P.M. without slowing down. We were moving at warp speed through the sleepy streets of suburbia late at night going 80 m.p.h. My Mother got a lead on them and turned into someone's driveway, threw the automatic into PARK, killed the engine, the lights and commanded all of us to HIT THE FLOOR!

Even though we all were down on the floor, hidden from view, it felt as though the station wagon glowed in the dark. It didn't help that she parked right under a street light.

There we sat, on the floor of our car, Mother, Sherry, Terrie, Suzanne, Danielle and me, parked in a stranger's driveway. Sherry had escalated whining to crying out loud. Suzanne, Terrie, Danielle and I sat on the floor in the back seat. I could see the three of them looking at me by the light from the streetlamp. They weren't afraid, just resolved to the lunacy of my mother.

No one made a sound except for Sherry's sobs.

After what felt like an eternity but in reality was about two to five minutes on my mother's impatient clock, she gave the all clear. She thought it was safe to venture back on the road and take my friends home thinking she lost the boys. My mother backed out the driveway slowly. It is a wonder the people who lived there didn't call the police on us. At the four way stop at the corner, there they parked. Rick and Eddie sat waiting at the intersection. When they saw our car, they rolled across in front of us, waved and turned in another direction. My Mother froze as if now they had us cornered. I did not wave back. I gave an inconspicuous head nod by way of acknowledgement. If my mother saw it I could explain it as a nervous twitch. The only one, besides my mother, who was terrified during the ordeal was Sherry. Sherry's sobbing, along with my mother's tirade, woke up my father when we arrived home.

My dad. He was so glad to hear my mother had not wrecked the car that he dismissed all of it until morning. He ran us all off to bed. Dad was the calm in the storm, although his sense of humor was a little thin that late at night.

That was almost thirteen years ago, and Rick called me, but my mother hung up on him.

I sat wondering if I was missing the station wagon or relieved it was finally gone.

I snapped back when Julia pulled into the drive-thru Daiquiri Shoppe. That's the second time tonight I was lost in a bubble. The drive-thru remained open 24/7. "This should help calm our nerves. The usual?" she asked me.

"Yes, make it an extra large rum with three limes." I said absentmindedly.

Kent and his two brothers, Kink and Kal, from the neighborhood owned and ran this Daiquiri Shoppe. These were some of the boys from the neighborhood who used to chase Suzanne and I around shooting us with rubber-band guns.

Kink stood at the window and took our order after exchanging pleasantries. Once he went to make our drinks, to go of course, Julia asked me, "Who names their kid, Kink? Is it short for something? Is it a nickname? That goes for Kal. What do you think?"

"I think it's late. If you have an inquiring mind, you should ask them. However, it might come across as insulting. Just go with it, please, for now, or he might decide to spit in your daiquiri and I'll get spit in mine by mistake." After Kink made our daiquiris, Kent brought them to us, in extra large, lidded go cups, handing us the straws. He asked me how my parents were as he rang us up.

Julia answered, "Her mother is the same." Kent smiled and gave us half off our bill by way of the neighborhood discount. Maybe he still felt bad over the rubber-band guns or because he liked looking right down Julia's blouse. I thanked him. As we drove away from the drive-thru window

Julia said, "I am glad I didn't ask him about the name thing. We might not have gotten the discount. So, what is it? Does every guy in your neighborhood have the hots for you?"

"No. It just helps that I grew up in a neighborhood where the boys outnumbered the girls about ten to one. At the time, they thought those were great odds. Time had a way of letting them learn how that worked out in our favor."

Chapter Ten

WE LEFT STAN'S after we got our things and agreed to meet later that morning at his office to see about finding the station wagon. Then he drove us to my house. It was five-thirty A.M. and the only sleep I had all night was the power nap at Club Bare Minimum. Stan told me he would start working on finding my mother's station wagon when he got to his office. Julia and I made coffee while we sat and waited to deliver the bad news to my mother about how her beloved station wagon was stolen. Dante had my car back in the driveway just like he promised, parked right in front of his patrol car. He had me blocked in.

While we waited to face my mother about the station wagon, Woozie, our housekeeper, arrived at her usual time to start work. She was surprised to see us.

"You're up early," Woozie said to me by way of a good morning.

"No, not up early, out late. We just got in." Julia answered a little too smart-alecky for

Woozie's taste.

"What are y'all up to?" Woozie started the interrogation looking at me.

"What are you doing here so early?" asked Julia by way of trying to avoid answering.

"Brandy knows why I gets here early. My son, Silas, brings me when he gets off his job. Not that I answer to you, Missy." Woozie was our housekeeper who had been with our family since my Grandmother gave birth to my mother. She started working at fifteen and was now close to sixty. She took in foster kids and was great with them. Nothing gets by Woozie.

Julia continued as if Woozie wasn't present. "Why do you feel you have to wait to tell Mommy the bad news in person about the car being stolen? I think you should just leave a note and call with good news once it's found." Every blue moon Julia has a good idea. Avoiding Dante and my mother was a double header, a two for one. I decided to leave a note.

When I finished I read it aloud for Julia and Woozie's benefit. *Mom, please use my car until I locate yours. I think someone stole it while we were at Charity Hospital. I'm out trying to find it. Love, Brandy*

"You got your momma's car stolen?" Woozie was looking at me with her head tilted so I could only see one eye. She looked like a parakeet when she did this.

"I'm hoping she will be more concerned about me being at Charity than her car missing."

"What was you doin' at Charity? You white people don't needs to go there unless you go and get yourself shot. If you not shot going in, you sure might get shot coming out." Woozie had turned her head and was giving me the other parakeet eye.

"We didn't get shot." I said to the bird lady.

"Your momma is gonna pitch a conniption fit, even if her car has done had it. That car is as old as dirt. Don't tell her I said that," Woozie said in "who dat" speak.

Woozie's secrets were always safe with me, just as mine were safe with her. She was there when I came home from the hospital and has always said to me that I was her favorite white child. I guess that makes her my favorite black mother. Woozie and I were careful not to offer that info to my mother or sister.

"You better walk and feed them dogs you brought home." Woozie was always moving while she talked, either washing, dusting, straightening, or picking up stuff. She was steady, not fast, not slow. She could get more done in a day than I could in a week. She set up the ironing board and started filling the steam iron with water from a go cup. She squeezed the rim to make a spout so the water didn't spill all over.

"Dis one you brought here, has done jumped up on da back of your momma's sofa, in da living room," she nodded her head toward the front of the house, "he done pulled down all your momma's nice drapes. Then she tried to catch dat little dog. It a good thing he run fast. He run so fast she couldn't sees where he run off to. I sees him go under da bed hiding."

"She didn't hurt Geaux Cup did she?"

"No. I tell your daddy where he hiding and your daddy gets him out. Geaux Cup? Give that dog a good dog name like Rex or Duke. What about King? I like King."

"Rex or Duke? King? Those sound like Mardi Gras names, not dog names." Julia interjected.

Woozie continued to iron as if Julia was not talking or even here. "And then, dat little dog goes and jumps up on your bed, after I makes it, and sleeps in da middle of them pillows. I tries to gets him off your bed but he hunkers down and growls at me."

Julia added, knowing Woozie was listening even if she didn't answer her, "Wait til her mother sees the one she's got stashed at Stan's office."

"Not that Stan boy who used to live up the block? He still dress up like a duck? Something not right about dat boy." Woozie said as she pressed a killer crease in my dad's work pants.

"Stan is an attorney now and he no longer

wears the duck costume. Woozie, help me out. Geaux Cup isn't growling, he's talking to you. These little dogs are talkers. Please feed my babies and let them out for 10-15 minutes after I leave. He's a lover not a biter. He'll follow you anywhere for a piece of cheese. If I let them out now, they will start barking and wake up my mother."

"Well, it sure sounded like he saying, 'I ain't gettin' off this bed' and, what kinda name is Geaux Cup for a dog anyway? I won't be calling dat dog Geaux Cup. He better not bites me. I don't need to be getting me no rabies shots and missing no work. You got too many dogs as it is. Most people only needs one dog. How come you needs so many?"

The idea of rescue was lost on Woozie. She, like Julia, didn't wait for answers to questions, just kept asking more. She and Julia had something in common, although I didn't think it was a good idea to point this out. I kissed her on the cheek, said thanks, and then I packed a bag of clothes. I packed enough for a few days in case I had to hide out at Julia's to avoid the wrath of my parents over the car. We high-tailed it out of there before my mother woke up and I had to explain the entire ordeal. We left Woozie swatting at the furniture with a dust cloth.

At Julia's we showered, changed, and I tried to catch a few winks. At nine A.M. I was wide awake and excited with the thought of meeting Jiff Heinkel today. My stomach went from butterflies to knots when I thought about how I was going to tell Dante about Jiff. Dante and I were close. My entire life with him flashed before me like floodgates were opened. We lived and grew up next door to each other. We played together since we were babies. He was my first friend, the first and only boy who told me he loved me.

I remember the day Dante told me he loved me like it was yesterday. I was five years old in kindergarten, and he was six years old in the first grade. Dante didn't go to kindergarten so the first day of school was the first time we had been apart since I came home from the hospital. At recess, as soon as he saw me come out of my class, he ran up to me and hugged me and said he loved me. He has never said it since, but we played together every day at school until the "incident."

It was one afternoon in the summer when the mercury ran a steady 100 degrees with 100% humidity. We didn't have central air conditioning then, just attic fans. The only thing the attic fans were good for was pulling more hot air into the house along with buckets of dust. I went outside to play where it was cooler. I was playing under the huge oak tree in my backyard when, Dante, and his brothers, Darryl, Dawson, Danny and Dennis called me over. They had a new game and they wanted me to play! They said they knew how to jump through the glass window without getting hurt. It was my great honor to go first.

They wrapped me in the heavy velvet drapes while they were still hanging from the rods in the living room in front of the window. They said I was going to be a Super Hero because I could jump through the glass. There was no jumping involved on my part. They pushed me through the plate glass and watched what happened while Dante waited his turn.

For the most part, it worked. Miss Ruth heard the glass breaking from the kitchen, ran to the living room and saw a small body wrapped in her good drapes suspended in the azalea bushes outside. I was not moving, and covered in broken glass. The azalea bushes in her unkempt flowerbed had snagged the drapes, keeping me from landing on the jagged shards lying below. I didn't have a scratch on me, but Ms. Ruth didn't know this. She screamed until she lost consciousness, fell on the floor and her head made a loud thumping noise. I bet it would have sounded a lot louder if I hadn't been wrapped in those velvet drapes. I was not sure what I was supposed to do in the drapes, and hearing the commotion outside, I started singing the song taught in my Brownie troop for times when we felt afraid:

"I have something in my pocket that belongs

across my face,
I keep it very close to me in a most
convenient place,
I bet you'll never guess it, if you guess a long,
long time,
So I will take it out and put it on
It's a GREAT BIG BROWNIE SMILE!"

When the police arrived I was still in the drapes. They found me by the muffled singing coming from inside. They unwrapped me and since I was taught never to speak to strangers, I wouldn't tell the officers my name.

The sirens from the medics and police cars along with their flashing lights did not go unnoticed in the neighborhood. Every Tuesday is hair day at my grandmother's house. She lived right across the street from Miss Ruth. My Grandmother and three of my great aunts got together on the same day, every week for the last 20 years, and did each other's hair. They washed, rolled, dried, and combed with military precision.

The process resembled a musical chair type scenario around the kitchen table. Having studied the process for years, I'm still no expert, but I think it went like this. First up, Lady A would be washed by Lady B, then was rolled by Lady C. Lady A moved to the dryer while Lady B was being washed by Lady C and rolled by Lady D, and so on. They moved along this production line until the dryer turned off and all heads were coiffured. One rolled under the dryer when one rolled out. The dryer looked like ones I'd seen in beauty salons, except this one was bigger, pink, and loud. This was a portable contraption and it sat on one end of the kitchen table. The dome was positioned over a chair placed under it with the chair facing away from the table. It should have been named a luggable not a portable since it could only be moved by a strong man, or two women. It folded up to a smaller version of itself for storage, about the size of a steamer trunk. The one under the dryer had an unobstructed view, not of the front door, but the kitchen wall and the stove. Once in the chair, the dryer's heating dome lowered over the head, covering it to almost the neck.

Each week, my grandfather resurrected, assembled, and set it on the table facing the stove, and away from the door. Then he disappeared to the inner sanctum of his garage and left the ladies to their hair. He reappeared the instant it went off and the final hair spray was being administered from what looked like an old bug spray can with a hand pump. The fog from the hair spray was so dense and hung over the entire kitchen so that when they stood up, you couldn't see their heads. This allowed my grandfather to covertly move in, disassemble the dryer and return it to its storage facility.

The commotion across the street at Miss Ruth's did not go unnoticed by the hair club. My Aunt Florence was in the middle of the wash cycle when the sirens rang out. With a towel wrapped around her head, she waited on the front porch of my Grandmother's house, wringing her hands, uncomfortable with the police, the sirens, and the unforeseen disruption in the weekly ritual. She had to get home to start dinner for Uncle Ervin and this setback would make dinner late.

Everyone came to see what happened. The Guidry boys, Kent, Kink, and Kal showed up on their bicycles from up the block. The twins, Ronnie and Donnie, who lived next door to the Deedlers poked through the glass while my friend Suzanne with her two younger brothers watched. A police car, fire truck and ambulance was parked in front of our house and the Deedlers next door when my mother returned in the green station wagon from her errands.

The only one who missed all the excitement was Aunt Nonnie. She was drying under the dome facing the kitchen wall and did not hear or see a thing.

After the police and the emergency team disbanded, my Mother blamed me for everything. I had allowed them to take advantage of me. She said I let them throw me through the window.

This caused Miss Ruth to scream, faint, and hit her head on the floor. It was all my fault that the ambulance and police came for nothing. Dante's youngest brother called the emergency number, not because they thought I was dead, but because this time they thought they killed their mother.

Suzanne, who knew better than to find my mother, went and found my grandfather. He carried me away from the fray and chuckled under his breath, so only I heard him tell me, "Thank God you aren't hurt. You need to be careful. Those boys play rough."

No one looked with humor upon it, least of all my mother. She told me, "Brandy, you are boy crazy. This will never end well." What was my mother talking about? I was five, almost six. I wasn't even sure at that age what the difference was between boys and girls. She went on, "Your dad and I have decided you can't play with boys anymore." My mother was on the warpath while setting the dinner table. My dad sat in his Lazy Boy, fully reclined. Most of my childhood memories are of him in this position with the newspaper opened in the middle over his face. I think it was my father's intention to sleep through our entire childhood, so he could get along with my mother.

I marveled at the fact that my mother, who like a duck on a June bug with everything else in life,

did not notice my Dad sound asleep. She concluded his lack of argument as agreeing with her.

Now, what was I going to tell Dante? I certainly didn't want the relationship his parents or my
parents had but that's all we both knew.

Julia was still sleeping with her eye mask on. I
got dressed and when I tried to wake her she
shoved me off.

"I need my beauty sleep to work tonight," her
muffled voice said coming from under the pillow
over her head. "Take my car." she added by way of
getting rid of me.

"No one looks at your face when you take off
your clothes." I said, but she was already asleep, or
she ignored me.

It was just as well. I needed a break from her
and Stan would be easier to work with if Julia
wasn't there. I grabbed the keys and said I would
give her an update after I met with him at his
office. I was off to see if anything had turned up
on the station wagon.

"Try not to let my car get stolen." Julia's muffled yell came from under the pillow before she
faded back into slumber land. I was going to do
my best not to get her cute, little, two seater,
Mercedes coupe hot wired.

Stan was at his office with Isabella, and he had
a couple of junior attorneys working when I got
there at 10:30. Stan let Isabella run around his

office on the floor. When we went to his private office, she jumped up into one of the client chairs across from him while he sat at his desk. I sat in the other chair. We both looked at Stan.

"She's a nice little dog. I like her. She goes to the door and barks at me when she wants to go outside. She's smart. If I didn't work so much . . ." he drifted off.

"Stan, every dog should have a boy. I have the perfect one for you." I was always positioning a rescue with a potential adopter.

He smiled yes, but his head shook no.

He told me he had already faxed a stolen vehicle report to a friend at NOPD.

"Please tell me the friend is not Dante." I really didn't want to strangle Stan, I liked him.

"There are brains behind this handsome face," he smiled at me, and for the first time I saw Stan as an accomplished attorney with the confidence he lacked as a boy. Stan had two junior attorneys who worked for him on a Saturday during Mardi Gras doing research on the Heinkel family. Old Stan had influence.

I smiled. He was a late bloomer, and it made me feel good to know he still carried the torch as I took that walk down ego lane.

"Get any rest? You had a long day yesterday," he asked.

"Not much, a little nap, but I feel okay. I

could use a cup of coffee. Have you found out anything on my mother's car or who shot Jiff Heinkel?"

"Coffee is in the break room. Right this way. All we have is coffee with chicory. Want some King Cake? I get Haydel's Bakery to deliver one every Friday in case we have to work the weekend. If we don't work, they stay fresh until Monday," Stan said slicing me a huge hunk of King Cake.

I nodded when I saw the purple, green and gold sugar on that cinnamon roll pastry. "I love Haydel's Bakery. I love King Cake. Don't leave me alone with it. I can eat the whole thing." I said. It ranked number one on my food failure list when dieting. Haydel's is my favorite and Randazzo's is a close second. You?"

"Traditional or filled?" Stan asked.

"Traditional, only traditional. I don't think filling them is an improvement," I answered.

"Me either. I'm a traditional kind of guy. Yeah I like those two the best. Why buy one anywhere else?" I nodded in agreement as I pushed a bite of that one-of-a-kind, sugary carnival tradition into my mouth. Stan made a fresh pot of coffee. We stood there eating King Cake waiting for the coffee to brew.

"On your Mom's car," he said, "I've got nothing so far, but Heinkel is another story. You know his family owns a lot of Plaquemines' Parish oil leases. We found out there is another guy down in the parish buying up oil leases from little old ladies and from successions. I am wondering why the Heinkel family isn't buying them when they become available. That would make the most sense. The Heinkels are well known and respected in Plaquemines. I think this other guy might be shaking down these individuals for their leases and transfers."

"Why do you think that?"

"Because the guy buying up all the single transfers or smaller transfers works for Ratty Tulhman, otherwise known as The Tool. Ratty is the sheriff down there. He has a fixer named Angelo who is the front man on all the sales. Both of these jamokes have less than stellar reputations. Our firm did some work on deporting a well known Italian we believe Tulhman was in business with. We think The Tool is making a run since his buddy was deported.

"The Tool? With a name like Ratty, people call him the Tool?" God, I was starting to sound like Julia.

"His name is Radcliffe and kids in school called him Ratty 'til he sent a couple to the hospital. No one calls him that to his face anymore. Most just call him Tulhman or Sheriff. I refer to him as Ratty if I'm in another parish," laughed Stan.

"Great. You think this is the guy who shot at Jiff and tried to get his dog?"

"It makes sense. These goons are small time and brainless. They start by hurting something that gets them no time if caught, like animal cruelty. They threaten some little old lady by saying they will kill her dog if she doesn't sell the oil leases. Unfortunately, the charges brought on behalf of animals don't get followed up on or addressed except to give the jerk a slap on the wrist, if that. There are no consequences for these guys to stop doing it. They terrorize the owner into believing it will escalate to them or someone in their family next. The fear of that works, and eventually, these goons will step up their game and hurt someone to get what they want or make their point."

He poured us each a steaming cup of Cafe Du Monde coffee as he continued with his findings, "The good news is the Heinkels are squeaky clean. Tulhman now owns almost as many oil rights and leases as they do, so I figure he's making his move. While the Heinkels have money and power on their side, Ratty has muscle and he doesn't mind using it. The two neanderthals who took your mother's car probably work for him, and I think they are the ones that shot Heinkel. Here's cream and sugar." He started to hand me the cup. He stopped, put both down, and pulled out a chair moving it under me saying, "Whoa! Brandy, you don't look so good. I think you better sit down."

"Good idea." I mumbled as my knees gave out and I collapsed into the chair. Once the blood felt like it was circulating again, I asked Stan, "What am I going to do? They know where I live."

"It's a lot to take in. Just take a deep breath, I'm here to help," and he handed me the cup of coffee.

"I am supposed to pick up Heinkel at the hospital after one o'clock this afternoon."

"What? Why are you doing that?"

"He asked me to. I don't know, it seemed like a good idea at the time. I was Duck Man. You know how that feels. The rush makes you think you can do anything! Besides, he didn't see me dressed as Duck Man, or my white gorilla sidekick, so he thinks he still wants to meet me. Imagine that?" I paused a minute thinking about it all. Maybe I was still riding the Duck Man high. I said, "I want to do something for him and Isabella, for those pets, for all the people and their pets these guys are hurting or killing. What can we do?" I paused for effect then added looking right at Stan, "Remember when you brought me that little dog? The one some guy was kicking when we were in high school. You said to find him a good home, and I did. Mine."

"I'm sure your mother remembers." Stan said

as he looked at me sideways. "I remember. That's unfair. Brandy, you know I can't say no to you."

I smiled. Just then one of the attorneys stuck his head in the break room and said, "I think they found the car, the station wagon."

"Great!" I jumped up. "Where? Can I go get it?"

"Uh, the police found it in the Desire Housing Project. It's been stripped and burned out." The young attorney read off the report.

Stan pushed the chair back under me. I sunk back down into it.

"Maybe it isn't the right car. Maybe they have it confused with another one, maybe . . ."

Stan read the sheet faxed from the NOPD and said, "It's the right car. The police don't make a mistake on an ID once they find a stolen car. They make a positive ID from the VIN number. This one seems like it was easier than most since it was left somewhere to be found. They rarely find them while they are still in once piece. Sort of like a shooting victim. When do the police find someone before they get shot? They don't. They find them after. It makes their job easier. By then the car isn't going any place and neither is the body." Stan handed me the faxed police report.

I read it and I caught my breath. Handing the fax back to Stan I said, "Look who wrote this. Recognize the name? He's Dante's partner, Joe."

"Let me see that. You're right and this is why it was found so fast. He knew where they took it. I know this guy. He grew up down in the parish with Tulhman. I bet he knows them or is working with them trying to intimidate you and Heinkel."

"People are lining up to kill me. My mother will be first in line. Then Dante, or his partner, Joe helping the guys who stole the car . . ." Every molecule in my body was trying to process what I learned. I felt overwhelmed. Stan took command and helped me up from the chair.

"I am not going to let anyone hurt you. I have an idea." I followed him to his office.

"Okay. You are going to pick up Heinkel as planned. Take him somewhere public, go to lunch somewhere and sit outside. If any of these guys see you, they will contact Tulhman or those guys who took your car. I want you decked out, high heels, wear something striking. Short, tight, low cut. You get the idea. For you that should be easy." Stan always with the compliment.

"I'm flattered, but are you crazy? We'll be sitting ducks. I don't have a gun, and I don't think Heinkel will be in any condition to protect me since he is being released from the hospital with," I paused for him to get the full effect, "*a gunshot wound.*"

"Don't worry. I'll be close by."

I didn't say it, but I'd feel better if Stan wore the Duck Man costume and brought the Quacker with him.

Chapter Eleven

I DON'T KNOW what had me more anxious, meeting Jiff to see where this was going or bumping into Ratty and his friends.

I changed into one of the outfits I grabbed that morning when leaving home. It was a snug fitting, red V-neck sweater dress and I wore my four-inch black pumps. Stan approved. I picked up Isabella and Stan followed at a safe distance behind me. I didn't know how I was going to push that wheelchair out to the car in these heels, so I parked Julia's Mercedes on the emergency ramp at the back of Charity Hospital on Cleveland Street. I left it with Isabella locked inside a few steps away from the ER entrance. I didn't think cars were stolen from the drop off ramp. It seemed like a good idea given the hostile environment of the neighborhood. Stan was parked down at street level where he could see me get out of the car. He had a good view up the ramp to see when I returned with Heinkel.

I found Jiff in his room sitting in the visitor's

chair by the window. He stood up when I entered. He was dressed in khaki slacks, a blue button down, long sleeve oxford shirt with one button open, leather tassel moccasins, and he looked ready to go. There was a folded up wheelchair against the wall. He said with a big smile, "Thanks for coming. I hope I am not keeping you from something or someone. You look too nice to be picking me up from the hospital."

"No, of course not, I said I would meet you. I'll bring you home or anywhere you want to go. I parked right outside and Isabella is in the car waiting for you."

"You look stunning," he said. I could feel my face flush at the compliment. "I would like to take you to lunch to thank you for all your help. I'm checked out of here and I'm all yours."

I liked the sound of that and felt lightheaded but went on, "That's not necessary, but we do need to talk about what is going on because of you."

"I hope I haven't complicated your life."

"I wouldn't say complicated, but some very interesting events have taken place over the last twenty-four hours I think you need to know about. First, I would like to ask you something," I ventured.

"Anything. Ask me anything." He sounded sincere.

I started to set up the wheelchair to give me something to do and said, "I am wondering why you picked me out of the crowd." I felt awkward and vulnerable and knew he was watching me.

"Here let me help you with that." He pushed a call button and an orderly appeared. "Maybe I should wheel you out," Jiff said. "I don't know how you plan to push a wheelchair in those shoes."

His smile only made him more handsome. I could feel my knees getting weak and for a second I thought he might actually have to put me in the wheelchair.

The orderly wheeled him out for me. "Where are your clothes, the tux you had on when they brought you in?" I asked.

"I called my assistant and asked him to bring me a change of clothes this morning. I sent the tux back with him. I don't think I'll be wearing that one again unless bullet holes in tuxedos become fashionable." He flashed his handsome smile.

Well, why didn't you ask your assistant to come take you home? Julia might be right and he might have a lady friend.

As if reading my mind, he said, "My assistant's name is Tom, and he takes his family to the parades on the weekends since he works late almost every night. I couldn't ask him to give up his day with the kids."

Was this guy for real? At the phone company

where I worked, if you needed surgery they wanted you to schedule it after hours and be back the following day.

At the hospital's ER entrance, the double doors opened automatically. Isabella spotted us and went crazy wiggling and barking for her owner. Jiff rose from the wheelchair. He thanked the orderly taking my arm to escort me to the driver's side of my car and opened the door for me. Once I was seated, he closed the door and walked to the passenger side and got in. Isabella was in his lap giving him doggie kisses in delight.

"What a good girl you are, Isabella. I hope you haven't given this lady any trouble," speaking to the dog. Then to me he said, "Nice ride. I didn't picture you as a sports car kind of girl."

"This isn't my car. That brings me to what it is I need to talk to you about. First, tell me why you picked me out of the crowd. Do I know you from someplace?" I started the car and headed for the Towers at the Lakefront.

"No. We, you and I, have never met. You might have heard of my family. My dad and my brothers don't do much to stay out of the news. My family is from Plaquemines Parish and all my brothers still live there. My dad and I are the black sheep since we chose to move and live in Orleans Parish. Dad moved to New Orleans after his mother died. I live in the Towers at the Lakefront, with Isabella. Oh, but you know that by now. Yeah. How do you know that?"

"No, no, no. You first. You answer a question for me, then I will answer one for you. Why did you pick me out of the crowd to kiss? Did I look good after you and your pals had been drinking all day?" I tried to keep it light.

"That's two questions. I didn't have anything to drink that day. There's a lot going on at my office and with my family so I didn't have any alcohol. I wanted to keep my wits about me. That's another story. Why you? One day I saw you bringing Sam that Schnauzer. Sam talks so much about Einstein that I can't get in a word to tell him how wonderful Isabella is. He said I should get a companion for Isabella and I should call you. Sam sings your praises about the good work you do for animal rescue and he thinks we have a lot in common."

Oh boy. Depending on how this turns out I'm either going to kiss Sam or kill him.

"I wanted to meet you so I asked Sam for your phone number. I was trying to figure out a good reason to call and ask you out. We never formally met, so I figured you would blow me off. Then I saw you at the parade and I thought I would take a chance on getting you to take a flower. I never planned on the kiss, it just sort of happened, like, like . . ." he was looking for the right word.

"Magic." I finished for him.

"Yes. Like magic." he said.

"I have never kissed a guy in a parade before. Flower or no flower." I said.

"You exceeded my expectations on our first encounter. I asked you to meet me at the end of the parade to ask you out. When I got shot all I could think of was who would know to take care of Isabella. It isn't what I had in mind when I asked you to meet me at the end of the parade."

"Well, how did you know I would meet you at the end of the parade?" I asked.

"If you felt what I felt during that kiss, I knew you would," he sounded sincere. "Now, it is your turn to answer my question. How did you find out where I lived or where to go find Isabella? Did Sam call you?"

"Okay," I said, "but this is a long story. Where are we going? Am I taking you home or somewhere else?" I forgot for a moment that I was supposed to stay very visible with Jiff per Stan's instructions. I guess he was following us. I forgot to check I was so mesmerized by Jiff.

"Take a right turn on Carrollton and go to Ye Olde College Inn. We can sit at one of the outside tables with Isabella. I know the owner, and the place is dog friendly."

College Inn was located in a school zone, across from the Seminary, near the two uptown universities and one block from Jesuit High School. It was a local favorite with an easy atmosphere and fun clientele. The place appealed to the business lunch crowd.

I told him everything about Charity and getting his name off the police report. I left out Dante and the Duck Man part. He had not seen or known me as Duck Man and I wanted to keep it that way. I might tell him if we got to know each other better. I didn't want to scare him off thinking I was a nutcase.

When I told him about his condo, Sam and the guys with guns, he started watching the rear view and side view mirrors and spotted Stan. "I see someone following us. Is that one of the guys you saw at my place?"

"No, he's an attorney friend of mine. His name is Stan and I have known him since we were kids. I went to him and asked for help when those guys showed up at your place. I wasn't sure how to get into Charity to get a message to you because I thought they would follow me. You had two guards, no, two guys in full SWAT uniforms at your door. He was afraid those guys who shot at you might be waiting for us when we left the hospital."

"My dad hired off duty police to guard my room. Dad is a little over the top with security." Jiff was still watching the rear view mirror trying to get a good look at Stan. "Is that guy following us your boyfriend?"

"No. He's a good friend." I said.

"What's Stan's last name? I think I know him." he said.

"You don't know him because he doesn't know you." I said.

"Fontenot. His last name is Fontenot, isn't it? He and his firm or his dad's firm, won that big tobacco law suit." Jiff said.

"It's his firm now, his father retired but still goes in a couple of hours a day. I guess he likes to stay busy. Yes, that's his last name. Stan Fontenot." I was feeling proud of Stan and protective of him as well. "I called Stan to help me after you were shot." I left off the part where I already had Isabella and I needed Stan to help me sneak into the hospital past the police.

We stopped at a red light and he made a friendly wave at Stan via his side view mirror. Stan nodded back. He said, "I remember that case. The Fontenot firm won beaucoup money on that class action. Everyone should have received a good settlement. Turn on Carrollton. College Inn will be on your left. I would like to thank him for helping you and me."

"I know where College Inn is, I live here, remember? I am not from way down in Plaquemines like you." I took a sideways peek at him and he was smiling. So was I.

He asked me how I got into rescue. I said, "I think I inherited a love of animals from my dad. I don't understand how people can give up their dogs after they have them. Don't they get attached? My dad and I get attached in about three seconds. I only rescue Schnauzers people no longer want and find a good home for them. Most of rescue work is fun and I meet wonderful, loving people who adopt the dogs, like Sam. People who surrender their pets always have a lame excuse for giving them up. Usually they aren't taking good care of their dogs so it's in the pets' best interest to find another home."

"Oh, I bet there are some doozies. What's your favorite, or rather least favorite, excuse?"

"Well, the real reason is that they are lazy and tired of owning or caring for the dog. The one that irks me the most would have to be, 'my new boy/girlfriend doesn't like dogs or is allergic to dogs.' I say get rid of the new boy/girlfriend. They're more likely to leave you before the dog will. I don't have any use for people who give up their pets and even less for anyone who hurts them. When you take a pet, it's a commitment for the life of the pet, and it should be given the best life you can afford to give them."

"Amen to that. What about Stan? Do you want him to join us?" he asked.

"I think Stan will go back to his office once he feels we aren't being followed. He is worried these guys may try to hurt me for helping you again. Those guys came to your place to try to grab Isabella, and then they were at the hospital and stole my car. Well, my mother's car."

"Great. Your parents hate me before they even meet me thinking I got their car stolen."

I smiled at the thought of him worrying about meeting my parents.

We parked and I was looking around for Stan. I didn't see him. I said, "I guess he is parking or circling the block looking for a space. We'll see him in a minute and I'll wave him over."

We were walking to an outside table when a van pulled up, the two who had been wearing red and green warm-up suits at the Towers were now in black and blue warm-ups and looking just as formidable. They jumped out and pushed Jiff, Isabella and me into their van and sped off. It happened so fast I couldn't even scream. I prayed Stan or someone inside the restaurant saw it.

Chapter Twelve

BLACK WARM-UP WAS driving and Blue was in the passenger seat twisted around facing us and pointing a gun. Isabella was growling.

"Shut that dog up or I will throw her out the window." Blue laughed like he just made the funniest joke. Black didn't respond.

"Let me have her," I said to Jiff. "I can get her to be quiet." I took Isabella and spoke softly to her while scratching her neck. This would always get my dog, Meaux, to settle down and be quiet and it worked on her back at the Towers. Meaux loved his neck scratched and I wondered if I would ever get to scratch him again. She quieted down, but was still tense and watched every move Blue made.

"What do you want with us?" Jiff asked. "You want me, not her and the dog. Let them go."

"Big man on campus back there wants us to let go of the broad and the dog," said Blue.

"I can hear him, Stupid," Black said to Blue. "No can do. She can ID us. Hey you two, see those blindfolds back there on the floor? Put them on and shut up!" he hollered over the seat.

"Okay, but I still hold the dog." I said.

"Who are you to be giving us orders?" asked Blue.

"Let her hold the dog unless you want to." Black said to Blue. Since Black seemed to have one ounce more brainpower than Blue he called the shots and drove.

"That mutt will get his soon enough." Blue said, a smug look to be a smile showing a few missing teeth. I bet this guy couldn't get a date for his prom. But then, he probably didn't graduate from school either.

"Why? What do you plan to do with her?" I stopped being afraid for me and was afraid for Isabella.

"The boss will decide. For now, both of you shut up and put on the blindfolds."

We did, but not before I took a mental snapshot of where we were headed. I could see out the front windows, but the back windows were filthy. I took a good look at the last place I saw and how fast we were going. Then I concentrated on the fact that we were going northbound on Carrollton. We just crossed Canal Street. Jiff and I inched closer as we put on the blindfolds and once mine was in place I hung onto Isabella with all I had. They were not taking her away from me without a fight. We leaned on the side of the van and into each other. Black and Blue started arguing about something and, for the moment. They ignored us.

We took a couple of right turns riding for about twenty minutes then we slowed down, stopping more than moving.

"Do you know where we are?" Jiff whispered into my ear. His mouth was so close I could feel his warm breath on my skin. It was arousing.

"We aren't far from where they grabbed us," I said. "I think we're still in the city. I think they're driving around in a big square to see if anyone is following us. Pay attention. Count to yourself and when they turn, make note if it is right or left, then count again." He didn't move away from my ear so he could continue to whisper to me. I felt him breathing on me. It would have been wonderful, especially with the blindfolds on, if we weren't in the van with the idiot twins.

I found it a little hard to concentrate with him so close. I managed for the next few minutes and sure enough, we kept making right turns as if going in a big square.

Jiff whispered, "I think we are back on Carrollton again. We are stopping longer so we must be on a big street with stop lights. If I counted right, we are back on Carrollton heading toward City Park."

We veered off to the right and rode for about another 10-15 minutes. "I think we're on

Esplanade." I told Jiff.

"Yeah, that's what I think too." he said.

We turned left and after a lot of stop, go and making right turns, Jiff asked me, "Where do you think we are now?"

"Somewhere in the French Quarter, I think, or right outside of it. We're stopping more than we're moving." I whispered brushing his ear with my lips. Sitting this close and touching him had me feeling all warm and tingly.

"I think so. I think we are near some sort of warehouse close to the river. Can you smell it?" he spoke in a low voice brushing his lips to my ear with his face next to mine.

What I smelled wasn't the river, it was him. It wasn't his cologne, or a fragrance from soap or detergent. It was him. He reached over touching me as he felt for my hand and held it. I wondered if I sent him a tantalizing scent in return. I had to concentrate.

"Yes, I smell the river, too," I said leaning on him and knowing my mouth was close to his lips which were still brushing my ear. If it wasn't for the eminent danger the three of us were in, I would have kissed him, blindfolded or not.

A faint sound I recognized brought me back to the van. "I can hear the calliope on the Steamboat Natchez, can you?"

"Yes, we can't be far from the French Quarter." he said.

I just wanted him to keep breathing and talking into my ear. I felt safe being so close to him.

We rode around for what I estimated to be about twenty minutes. Then, we slowed down, stopped for a minute, and I could hear a door opening. It sounded like an overhead warehouse door ratcheting up.

The van pulled forward and stopped.

Once I heard the door closing I got very cold. "I think we're in the Ice House on Decatur" I said.

I heard the front doors open, then the sliding door of the van they pushed us in. Someone was grabbing my arm and pulling me out. I held fast onto Isabelle but someone pulled her away from me and she yelped. "Don't hurt her, give her back to me," I demanded. Someone slapped my face, and tied my hands behind my back. When Jiff started to tell them not to hurt me, I heard what sounded like him getting punched and a stifled groan. They threatened to put another bullet in him if he didn't shut up. They pushed us down on the floor and tied us together sitting back-to-back. I heard them lock the door and their footsteps walking away. I could hear Isabella barking. She wasn't far from us.

Jiff asked me, "Are you okay?"

"Yes, I'm fine. Are you? How's your arm?" I worried they ripped his stitches when they punched him.

"My arm hurts where they hit me. I think it's starting to bleed a little. It's not bad, I think we're alone, don't you?" he sounded strong, confident.

"Yeah. Maybe. They're here somewhere. I don't know if they can hear us. I think we're locked in somewhere. I heard a door open, close and lock. It sounded like it was locked with a key. I think we are in some old warehouse, but we can't be totally closed in. Listen."

"I heard them walking off for a good bit. I can hear car traffic and Isabella whining," he said.

"We must be in some old office or room where the walls don't go all the way up to the ceiling. They could be watching us." I said and shivered at the thought.

"Yes, I think you're right. I just heard a river-boat horn. If this isn't the old Ice House, then we must be somewhere on the river just outside the French Quarter near it. I know Radcliffe Tulhman is behind this. He wants my family's oil leases and he has terrorized a lot of old people into signing theirs over for a song. I'm guessing your friend, Stan went back to his office."

"I hope Stan saw us get pushed into the van and called the police. I thought they would be here by now." I worried Stan might have missed our abduction.

I was afraid of what they would do to Isabella

and Jiff. Anger boiled inside me. I knew I had to control it and use it to help get us out of here. He said his arm was bleeding. They had been rough with me, I could only imagine how rough they were with him. If he lost too much blood in his weakened state, he might pass out. I kept my voice low and spoke calmly with a confidence that was for him, not me. I told him to control his breathing and try to relax so the bleeding would slow down. After a few minutes I felt his body relax some against my back.

After awhile, someone unlocked the door and came into the room. One of his thugs pulled off our blindfolds and I saw what could only be Ratty Tulhman. Stan was accurate in his description of him, but way too nice. Ratty was sinister. His beady eyes looked me over. He leered at me sitting on the dirty floor with my skirt hiked up to my hips. His slimy lips contorted into what I assumed for him, was a smile. He looked like he wanted to eat me alive.

"Let her and the dog go. Whatever it is you want, I'll give it to you," Jiff said.

"Well, well, well. Now we're singing a different tune," a sleazy voice matched the rodent like features of his face. "Now, I don't need you to give me what I want, I'm just going to take it. I think your dad and brothers will give me anthing when they find out you went missing. What do you think?"

"Tulhman. I should have known you were behind all this. So shooting me wasn't enough? You want our oil leases. Do you really think if you kill me that will coerce my family into signing them over?"

"Sure. This time we'll finish the job on you. Since you didn't get the message when you were shot. Your daddy won't want to lose anymore sons," Ratty was smirking.

"What about her? My dad doesn't even know her. Let her go."

"Nobody knows her. Joe said after she kissed you at the parade, her cop boyfriend won't be looking for her either. She won't be missed."

This confirms Dante's partner Joe knows this guy. Where, oh where was Stan. I hoped he saw us get thrown in the van. I heard a phone ring and Fat Black-Warm-Up-Suit came to get Ratty.

"Don't go away. We'll come back after we feed the pit bulls. Oh, your dog is going to be their dinner," he said mocking in a cordial voice as the three of them walked out of the room leaving our hands tied but the blindfolds off. We were in a room with meat hooks and the biggest butcher knives I'd ever seen.

One of the men asked Ratty, "C'mon boss, when can we have a little fun with them?"

"You can do whatever you want on your way

to dump them in the East," he answered. As Ratty closed the door I saw the other one putting Isabella in a fenced cage next to cages of pit bulls. The pits were looking her over. I felt bile rising into my mouth. I choked back the urge to vomit. As soon as they were gone, Jiff said to me. "I'm so sorry I got you into this."

"No time to be sorry. We need to get out of here." Now that the blindfold was off, my mind was processing where we were and it was about to come up with a plan. I could see the walls were only nine or ten feet high. Typical old office construction. "How far can you stretch your arms backwards away from you?"

"A little, I think. Why?"

"If you can extend yours back far enough I might be able to step through mine and yours. Then I can untie us. You will have to stretch as far as you can, though. How far do you think you can stretch before it hurts your arm?" Before he could answer I said, "I'm double jointed. Not a talent I can make money on, but now is a good time for it to come in handy."

"I'll stretch as far as I have to, if you think you can get us out of this." With that he was pushing his arms backwards from his body while we remained seated. I got into a squatting position staying as close to the floor as possible and moving our hands away from him and under my feet. We struggled a minute but then I got them where I could ball up and step back, getting both feet through both sets of hands. I could hear him wincing in pain. With both sets of tied hands now in front of me on the floor, I told Jiff we had to stand and he had to walk backwards. This was more difficult but we managed to get on our feet. I spotted a rusted sharp corner of a support beam and used it to cut through the zip tie.

"I'm glad these bozos didn't use handcuffs. We would've been screwed." After mine were off, I cut through Jiff's. Once we were both free, we took in the situation. The walls did not extend to the ceiling, but there was nothing to stand on to help us climb over.

"How bad is the pain in your arm? Do you think I can stand on your shoulders?" He looked a little pale. There was blood on his shirt but not a lot. "If I stand on your shoulders, I think I can get to the top of that wall and get over it."

"Let's do it."

I took off my shoes and put one foot on his bent leg while he crossed his arms to help me up, and then I worked my way up to his shoulders. He was putting on a brave face, but I saw him wince from the pain in his arm. "Do not look up my dress." I said as I used my hands to walk up the wall into a standing position.

"I wouldn't dream of it. What are you going to

do when you get to the top? It is a good drop. Don't hurt yourself."

"Oh, oh, my God. Oh my God!" I tried to keep the panic in my voice to a very loud whisper. I began squirming around on his shoulders trying to get as far away from it as possible. Jiff started staggering around stepping awkwardly back and forth trying to balance me and keep me from doing a high dive into the concrete floor. There it stood on high fuzzy legs on top of the wall. A big, fat, flying roach sat right where I wanted to put my hands and climb over.

I leaned as far away from the roach making Jiff step to keep his balance. I pulled myself along the wall opposite from the direction Jiff was moving in.

"What is it? What's wrong?" by now he stepped back and forth erratically trying not to lose his footing and keep me steady.

"There's big roach on top the wall," I was starting to sweat.

"Well, just shoo him off."

"No, no, no, no, no, no. He will fly right at me. Walk down the wall Walk. Walk. Walk faster. We have to get away from him." I tried to lean away from the roach using the top of the wall and pulling us away from where he sat. His whipped his antennae around letting me know he knew where I was and he was taking aim. "Go further up on the wall away from him." He started sidestepping to get me to another section of the wall. I felt the urge to jump off his shoulders. I felt like jello inside. A roach, a big hairy roach stood between me and escape. This was all my mother's fault. This roach phobia.

"Not that way, the other way, that way," I said pointing as if he could see my hands while I stood on his shoulders. "Get. Get. Get behind him. Maybe if he doesn't see me he won't fly."

"What is it with you and roaches? We live in New Orleans." He struggled but kept his balance with me and moved us away from the roach. I leaned away further and faster than his feet were moving but I didn't fall.

"It's a long story." I now worked my way down the wall, opposite to where the roach faced. "If he flies and lands on me, they won't have to kill me. I'll die of a heart attack."

"What about the drop on the other side? You aren't worried about that, and you are worried about the roach?" he sounded confused.

"Well, you are about six feet and I am five-foot-nine inches so the drop, if I can hang onto the top, will only be about five feet. I think I'll be okay. Oh my God! Oh my God! The roach turned around and is looking at me again. I have to go for it now before it starts flying."

Working as fast as I could, I put both hands on

top of the wall and pulled myself up halfway to my waist then swung a leg over, to straddle it. The roach made me move at warp speed. I sat straddling the wall when Jiff looked up. "I told you don't look up my dress!" I hissed in a loud whisper.

"I can't help it. I'm watching you and I can sort of see up your dress, but I'm not looking up your dress."

I had to just go with it, the roach, looking up my dress, all of it. Just as I swung my other leg over, and hung there bent in half hanging on the wall at my midsection, feet hanging on the side to freedom, that dang roach starting flying. I had to use both my arms to support myself. My plan needed both arms to hold onto the top of the wall to walk down it with my feet and reduce the falling space to a minimum. I could not let go with even one hand to defend myself from the aerial attack of the roach. It was all I could do not to scream as it closed in on me in a circular flight pattern. The roach flew in circles making big loops gearing up for his grand finale—to hit me right in the face. I could see it coming and was helpless to do anything about it.

On the last fly by, Jiff jumped up and caught the flying thing in his hand with his good arm. He threw it to the floor and stepped on it. Done. Awestruck that someone would do that for me made me want to climb back over the wall and kiss him. I could only look at him and mouth a thank you in a whisper.

"Well, you said if it landed on you, you would die of a heart attack and I would like to kiss you at least one more time. Next time, I'll kiss you like I mean it," he smiled. My hero.

With the threat of the roach behind me, I inched my way down the wall on my chest as far as I could go, hung by my hands so the full length of my body was reaching the floor and made the drop with a soft thump. I hurried over to unlock the door.

"They locked it with a key and the key is not here." I said to him through the door. I fought off the panic inching up my spine. Any minute they would be back and start what I didn't want to think about.

"You go. Get out of here and go for help." he said in a low voice through the door.

"I don't want to leave you." I felt tears filling my eyes.

"Look, if one of us gets out, that person can get help. You have to go." He added, "Take Isabella if you can."

Now, I had to get out of here and bring back help for him.

"O.K. I'll take her. Toss me my shoes over the top. Do it one at a time so I can catch them and not make any noise. I might need them if I get out of here." Jiff tossed one up, high so I could see where it was going to land. I caught it before it hit the floor. "OK, now the other one, just like that."

Once I had my shoes I put my hand flat on the door as a way of parting. I didn't know it but he did the same on the other side. I held the shoes and quickly moved to get Isabella out of the cage. "Shh, shh, shhhh." I was lowering the pitch with each Shh to get all the dogs, especially the pits, to settle down. The pits started to growl and show their teeth. In the loudest whisper I started singing, "How much is that doggie in the window?" It relaxed them and they laid back down. Charming dogs is my gift, what can I say? If it worked on men like it did on dogs, then Julia would have a run for her money! I wanted to let the pits out, but couldn't take the chance they might attack Isabella or me. They all had scars on their faces, necks and bodies. If I had to guess, these were the winners of dog fights. Losers were left to die or were shot. Isabella probably would be used as a bait dog. Schnauzers were feisty and would fight back if attacked, even though they would lose and be torn apart. Participants in dog fighting rings used small terriers to fire up their pits for the big fight. I discovered this is only one of the many abusive and cruel things people can and will do to animals when I got into rescue. Little, if anything, is ever done to help these animals or prevent it from happening. Dogs don't vote, so politicians could care less. It's disgusting. It wasn't the pit bulls' fault that someone makes them fight for their lives. What kind of person does this to another living thing?

Answer. Someone like Ratty Tulhman.

This is just another way he used to gain advantage over someone else.

Once the pit bulls were quiet I opened the wire door to Isabella's cage. She started squeezing through the opening as I unlatched and opened the gate. I closed the gate and secured it to give the appearance she could still be in there.

I made my way along the walls trying to stay in the shadows and darkness holding Isabella and my shoes. We were in the abandoned Ice House on Decatur. Big ice tongs and every size ice pick and hook hung up on racks suspended from the ceiling. Big freezers lined all the walls. They could kill someone in here and store them forever before anyone found them. They put us in a walled-off area used as old office space.

I inched along the wall holding Isabella, looking for a way out. I found a fire exit. I took a deep breath and pushed the door bar open hoping that the fire alarm was the silent one to the fire department. Of course, it wasn't. It blasted the alarm over what sounded like a hundred Klaxon horns. I didn't wait to see if the Fashion Twins would follow. I knew they would when they figured out one of us got out through the exit. Outside I saw the address, 2200 Decatur Street. I was very close to the French Quarter.

I took off running as fast as I could toward Esplanade. I figured if I could get there before they caught up with me I could get lost in the Saturday night crowd. I still held Isabella and the shoes, afraid to put her down. I didn't know if she would follow me or if she might run back to Jiff. I ran barefoot. At Esplanade Avenue I ran past the Mint and across to the Old French Market. I saw no one around. I ran through to the end of the French Market toward Cafe du Monde when I heard "Stop, you bitch!"

"Are they talking to you or me?" I asked Isabella as I tried to pick up my pace and tighten my grip on her. I stopped thinking about my feet even though they were starting to hurt. I prayed I wouldn't step on glass or a lit cigarette butt.

I searched everywhere looking around for a cop, a cop car, anyone who looked like he or she could help me. Everyone I saw was a little lit up and into his or her own party. A couple of guys invited me to join them but they were in no shape to help. These were happy drunks not fighting drunks. I continued running down Decatur pushing past the crowd of tourists holding drinks in go cups. They were having a good time and did not care or get physical over me pushing and bumping into them. Even the ones who were annoyed at first would lighten up when they saw the dog. Isabella was my ticket to make as much time as I could before they caught up with me. Everywhere was crowded with tourists until I got to St. Ann Street and hooked a right to hide in a doorway. I had to share the occupancy with a homeless man sleeping in the recessed entry. He didn't seem to mind or wake up, but he smelled to high heaven. I stepped over him and stood in the darkest corner behind him. All I could think of is how much worse the stench must be for Isabella given her sensitive dog nose. I put Isabella down and she moved as far away from the man as possible. She realized we were hiding, and sat very still next to me while I tried to catch my breath without breathing in the stench in the doorway. I didn't want to stay here too long. If Black and Blue made the turn with me, that would put them too close. I had put a good distance between us at the French Market. I slipped my heels on, picked Isabella back up and peeked out from the darkness. No thugs. My feet were still hurting but in the heels they were starting to numb. I had to put them on, there was glass everywhere and it was a miracle I hadn't stepped on any running in my bare feet. That would have really slowed me down.

I had no leash so I had to carry Isabella. I stepped out of hiding and continued at a fast walk, trying not to draw attention to myself.

Where St. Ann meets the back of St. Louis Cathedral, a bride and groom were leading a second line. They must have come from a reception at Muriel's on Jackson Square. I fell in line with them. It was a good cover to get lost in a crowd of well dressed people who all knew each other. If it happened I needed help and some good Samaritan in the crowd came to my aid, chances were his friends in the crowd would join in thinking I am one of the invited guests. Everyone around me wanted to pet Isabella. No one asked what's a dog doing at a wedding. Hey, it's the French Quarter. Anything and everything seems like a good idea with liquor. I joined them second lining until we were near Pirates Alley where I peeled off and worked my way over to Bourbon Street. Bourbon Street is crowded fifty-two weekends a year and was especially packed this every night during Mardi Gras. I squeezed through the crowd and kept moving down Bourbon Street toward St. Ann. At the corner there are two popular night clubs. One is Oz and across the street is The Bourbon Pub. Both places have stages with live performances turning into dance clubs afterwards, and both are gay clubs. The performers dress and sing as celebrities or dance to a generous crowd of tippers. I had come to Oz once to see my hairdresser, Allen, who used to perform in his Marilyn Monroe persona. I took a chance on Allen being there performing, and then remembered Woozie said her son Silas worked the bar at Oz. I am sure Woozie did not know this was a gay bar and I certainly didn't want to be Silas when she found out. I didn't know if Silas was gay, but he was an extremely good looking guy. I'm sure he made good tips serving drinks. Still, I saw no police officers anywhere. They were all managing parades and traffic.

I had to take my chance at Oz and hoped one of them, either Silas or Allen, would be there. My other option might be to find Julia and where she worked tonight. The clubs she worked were all at least eight to ten blocks away, closer to Canal Street, and she could be anywhere on Bourbon. Julia worked as a bouncing stripper at one of the six Bare Minimum Clubs owned by a local sleaze bag, Joey Feene. She went where Pinky sent her for the night or part of the night. That would take too long to find her and those guys would catch up with me. I headed through the door when a big white security guy wearing leather chaps and a cop style black leather hat, stopped me and asked for the cover charge. He stood about six-foot-four, about 220 lbs. of rippled muscles with shoulders almost as wide as the doorway with his ass completely exposed. I had no purse, no money, only the dog.

"I have no money with me. I just got away from two guys chasing me."

"Oh, honey, if I had two guys chasing me, I'd let them catch me."

"Not these two. They are going to hurt me. They kidnapped me and my friend and took us to the Ice House. I managed to get out with the dog. Is Silas here working the bar? I know him and his mother."

"No one named Silas at the bar, guess again." Now, he's not so friendly. He reached around me taking cover charges from men entering in all stages of dress and undress.

"What about Allen?"

"No Allen either."

I felt panic creeping in. What was Allen's stage name? I couldn't remember.

"Allen does Marilyn Monroe and Liza Minnelli impersonations."

"They all do Liza or Marilyn," he added, "eventually." He continued to reach around me and take cover charges. "I think Marilyn ran off with JFK." This brought a chuckle from the people entering and filing past me.

"Silas is a big, black, handsome guy, about six-three or six-four, great body, long straight black hair. He is about twenty two." Security kept reaching around me taking five dollar bills from entering patrons as if I wasn't standing dead center in the doorway. I worried he would ask me to move or leave. He could say he was going to call the police but I already knew what sort of empty threat that was. Police do not rush to a gay club. Seeing my options fading, and I don't even know why I said this to a big, white, gay dude with his ass fully exposed, "His Dad was a Tchoupitoulas Indian and he was his spy boy."

Security stopped taking cover charges, looked at me and said, "Oh. You mean Big Chief! He is upstairs in the dressing room. He isn't a bartender, he is a performer. Wait a minute," he stopped the next patron trying to enter, "right this way. Lady with a dog, coming through." He ushered me in and pointed toward a dark back area of the bar.

I wasn't ready for Silas to be Big Chief, gay, a dancer, or a singing, gay, Indian dancer, but I was running out of time and options. As I passed through the entrance, I glanced back up the street. Black and Blue were about a block away on St. Ann street looking in doorways. They hadn't spotted me yet.

"See those two coming up the block? Those are the guys chasing me. Please don't tell them I'm here." I said as I pressed past security. It was crazy crowded inside and dance music blasted so loud it made my eardrums start humming. The place was packed with standing room only. Wait staff hustled taking orders for last minute drinks or to get tabs paid out as the emcee announced Drag Queen Bingo was wrapping up, and the live performances were starting. All the patrons inside were dressed in outrageous costumes of every description. Some of these costumes were extravagant and eloquent, while others were extreme in their brevity and nudity. A gal stood in the midst of a group of men who were all looking at her up close and touching her all over her body. I thought she had on the tightest costume ever made, until I realized it was body paint. She had on no clothes. The guys were touching her to see if she is really nude. All that stood between her and the crowd is body paint. It looked like she was completely dressed in a Bat Girl outfit. I tried to figure out who worked in this club as waiters, then I spotted someone carrying a drink tray and asked where was the dressing room. He ignored me. To the next waiter rushing past me, I asked, "Where is Big Chief?"

"Right this way, honey." The tall, very thin, person with a tray stopped when he heard Big Chief and pointed to a wall painted black. I didn't see it at first but there was a door painted black like the rest of the wall. He said, "Go through there and up the stairs. His dressing room is at the top." I felt like Alice in Wonderland entering the rabbit hole. I went through the door, up a flight of stairs into a dressing room full of men wearing makeup, lots of makeup, some walking around only in pantyhose, sheer pantyhose. I wasn't sure where to park my eyes.

"Brandy?" I stood face to face with Liza Minnelli who had a voice like Allen, my hairdresser.

"Allen? Is that you? I need help. I am looking for Big Chief. Is he here?" Allen became enraptured with Isabella. He rattled on oblivious to my plight, "Oh, I could use this little darling and be Judy Garland as Dorothy singing *Somewhere over the Rainbow*. How great would that be? Here at Oz?" There was no redirecting his focus back to me. He was on a tear. Allen took off for somewhere over the rainbow.

"Brandy?" Silas came over when he heard me ask for Big Chief.

"Silas?" I asked the only big, partially dressed, creole man there. "Brandy! What brings you here, girlfriend?" He ran over dressed in his loin cloth and gave me a big bear hug and kiss. Silas is a gorgeous man with a tall chiseled body. He wore his hair, long and straight with two braids, one on either side of his face. Each braid had a feather attached to the end which dangled below his chin. His eyes were large, round and emerald green. He didn't need any makeup on his face other than the war paint. He was surrounded by other male performers in various stages of undress. One performer stood in front of a mirror putting on makeup, wearing only fishnet pantyhose and nothing else. There would be no panty lines showing with those fishnets. There was hair on that part of his body poking through the diamond shapes in the mesh. I wanted to ponder this hairy dilemma. Would *Nair* work on his problem? I didn't have time. Jiff was counting on me, and hopefully Ratty was not taking my escape out on him. At least the two following me weren't back there using him as a punching bag but that would change if they didn't catch me.

Along one wall was an extra long sofa with an enormous woman sitting there sewing velcro onto costumes. She took up over half of it so it looked like a love seat under her.

"Hey everybody! This is Brandy, a family friend. Brandy, this is everybody!" Silas announced. All the performers turned, smiled, waved or blew me a kiss, then went back to getting ready for their performances. Allen had Isabella and was brushing her with a soft hairbrush. When he finished brushing, he started tying bows on her collar.

The seamstress finished sewing and began gluing Lee Press On nails on one of the performers who was dressed in a long, sequined ball gown. She sat down across from the seamstress, who had to completely extend her arms to reach across her enormous bosom to work on the nails.

"Silas, I thought you were a bartender here. Woozie told me you tend bar and you get good tips. I'm in a tight spot and I'm really hoping you can help me."

"I do get good tips and I sort of let her think I'm a bartender." He leaned over and into my ear said, "My stage name is Cole. I don't like anyone knowing my real name here. It might get back to my mother." He started to put on his large, tall and wide head dress of what looked like 10,000 feathers. He added in my ear, "I'm straight and I don't let anyone here know that either."

"Look, Silas, uh, I mean Cole, I am here because I need help."

"You name it dah'ling, Whatever you need, you're family," he answered while continuing to dress, putting on his moccasins and more war-paint.

"These two very bad, mean guys kidnapped my friend, and Isabella," I said pointing to her, "and me. They took us to the Ice House on Decatur. I managed to get out with the dog but they're going to kill my friend, uh, my uh, the guy I was kidnapped with."

Cole stopped dressing. "What? Who? What do you need me to do?"

"I got out and ran here and couldn't find a

policeman anywhere. I need to call them to go there and help me, or at least call . . . I need to call my friend Dante or Stan."

"The police don't come down here as a rule . . . unless they are gay and out of uniform. That guy over there in the policeman's uniform is part of my Village People act, but he's no cop. Your friend Dante comes down here a lot. Did you see him downstairs when you came in?"

"Dante? What? If he is here, it must be because someone called in a 911 call. You must be mistaken."

"Oh, no, I'm not mistaken, but it seems you are. The last few weeks I've seen him come in here really late, after he's off duty and out of uniform." Silas looked skeptical about giving me this information. "Most cops are homophobes, so unless they bat for our team, they don't even come down here when we call them with a legitimate reason, like a shooting. I thought he lived next door to you. Oh, don't worry, he's probably a pitcher, not a catcher, or he bats for both teams."

"What?" How could men, gay or straight, be so cavalier about love. I thought my head was going to implode, just then, we all heard what sounded like chairs flying downstairs and people yelling something. One of the performers, a very tall person who looked to be 250 pounds, dressed as a butterfly, came running up the back stairs into the dressing room saying "Two big brutes just ruined my act. They are downstairs turning the place inside out." She sat down at a mirror between me and the door.

"Oh God, I think they're here. The two guys who kidnapped us followed me. Are they wearing black and blue warm-up suits?"

"Yes, that's them. Their suits are very ill fitting. They must be off the rack," said the Butterfly. While large, she moved gracefully and seemed to be very light on her size sixteen feet.

"Is there somewhere you can hide Isabella and me or get us out of here until I can call the police or Stan?" I asked looking around the small dressing area for a hiding place.

"You bet. OK, listen up everyone! Brandy here is in trouble and we need to hide her. Quick, Lola, she is about your size," he said to the one getting the Lee Press on Nails. "Get her one of your outfits with the wig, a black wig. Brandy, strip down. You need to get into this pronto."

What happened in the next sixty seconds was nothing short of miraculous.

"Liza, give me the dog," Silas said to Allen.

Everyone sprang into action with a specific task in mind. Lee Press on Nails, aka Lola was helping me undress, removing my shoes, another person was twisting my hair up to a bun and bobby clipping it so that Lola could put the wig and headpiece on me.

Cole said, "Too late for a costume, someone, give her a kimono. Here, sit here, Brandy. Camille," to the person wearing the butterfly costume complete with wings, "put gobs of makeup on her." Camille began to move deftly around my head applying my face with severe theatrical make up. She flitted around my face, then Voila! I had on fake lashes, purple eye shadow and enough rouge to paint a STOP sign. Camille used the same color on my mouth which gave me the appearance I just had 40 pounds of collagen injected into my lips. I didn't recognize myself. Somebody was putting my arms into a kimono while someone else was pulling off my dress. Cole gave Isabella to the seamstress and said "Momma, hide her in your secret place." Big Momma opened the top of her dress and snuggled little ten pound Isabella between her huge bosoms. Isabella looked shocked but kept quiet and still.

"Lola, give me your black wig and that Vegas showgirl head piece." said Cole.

"Now, act like a drag queen," Cole said to me. "Sit up straight, and be demonstrative with every move. Overtly demonstrative. If you have to speak to one, make everything over the top, gestures, words, actions. Got it?" He cleared a spot at one of the lighted mirrors and I started adding makeup to my face like last minute touches. While I did this,

Cole and the guy dressed as the sailor found the biggest headpiece I had ever seen outside of an Endymion parade with more feathers on it than I had ever seen in one place. It took two people, to lift it, set it and strap it to my head. When it was on my head it sat five feet high and weighed a ton. It took an enormous amount of effort to keep its weight from pulling my head forward or backwards and taking me with it to the floor. "Here move your head like this" he said showing me how to move my head looking side to side so that the feathers were invading the space behind me and keeping anyone from getting too close to me.

"No, not that much, you'll fall over." Just as he said it I fell backwards, the headpiece taking control. He and Lola caught the headgear and me, righting us both. "It takes a little getting used to. Less is more. Just move your arms and look right, then left. Slowly. Let the feathers do the work. Just move your arms around like you are stretching and are warming up for your act."

I started doing ballet arms, when Cole added, "Think Drag Queen, bigger, more dramatic, like so." He moved his arms in large circles in front of his face and chest while moving his head slightly side to side. "See?" When I did it, the head piece had feathers tossing about everywhere. "That's it, he said." We could hear what sounded like King Kong coming up the stairs. "Showtime." said Cole.

Black and Blue busted in and all the performers started cackling like a gay hen party. Every performer was aghast in one way or another, but all of the performers responded to the intrusion in over the top fanfare. Camille whispered in my ear, "Keep looking into the mirror at them. Don't look straight into their faces." They went from person to person checking for me. When they got within one person away from me, Cole stepped in front of them blocking them from passing and said, "If you boys are looking for some fun you came to the right place."

Black said to Blue, "C'mon, she's not here. Let's get outta this butt hut."

Chapter Thirteen

THEY BUMBLED OUT of there and all the queens in the dressing room started talking at once. I started shaking. I said to Cole, "They're going back to The Ice House and hurt or kill Jiff. I have to do something. I need a phone to call Stan."

"Here is the phone. Dial away." Lola handed me the phone and added, "You bitch, you look better in that headdress than I do," and then smiled at me. Silas and the Sailor started to remove the monstrosity from my head.

I dialed Stan at the office. It was late on Saturday night. I don't know why I thought he would be there, but he picked up. "Hello, Stan Fontenot."

I couldn't talk fast enough, "Stan, where have you been, didn't you see us get pushed into the white van? We were blindfolded and taken to . . ."

"What?" he cut me off. "What happened, where are you?"

"That's what I'm trying to tell. Ratty Tulhman had his two goons kidnap Jiff, Isabella and me. His guys took us to the old Ice House on Decatur. Jiff helped me get out of there so I could go for help. I took the dog and I don't have any money, so I'm at Oz on Bourbon Street with someone . . . I mean where I know someone who . . . works here. I'm calling from his phone. Ratty's two big thugs chased me and came in here looking for me. Those two just left, and now are probably going back to the Ice House to hurt and kill Jiff. Ratty said they were going to kill me too." It all spilled out in one breath.

"I saw you park and get out. I was looking for a parking spot and lost you. I called the police to file a report but they won't write up a missing person until you are gone for twenty-four hours. I didn't see the van. I'm so sorry. I drove around for hours looking for you. I came to the office hoping you would call me here if you got a chance. I'm on my way. Stay where you are."

"Tell him to meet you at the Ice House," Cole said. "I have an idea. Follow me."

I gave Stan the exact address of The Ice House, and told him I was going back there now with help. I added I would be hiding or waiting in a safe place.

"I'll call the police, bring backup and meet you there. Brandy, I'm so sorry. Be careful." and he hung up.

Lola handed me a slinky black, backless gown.

I put my own shoes back on as the ones Lola put on my feet were a size twelve and I didn't think I could walk in them.

Cole shouted for everyone dressed to follow him. We went downstairs and he got up on stage with the other Village People and performed *Macho Man*. The crowd went wild. Once he got them revved up, he got on the microphone and said, "All you macho men out there, let me see your hands." Most of the room raised their hands. "OK, who wants to go to an all macho man party where the drinks are free!" He yelled over the excited crowed. More people raised their hands, including the women there. That's when I spotted Dante, or someone who looked like him in the crowd. No. I must be delirious from lack of sleep. He didn't recognize me in Lola's get up. I felt as if someone knocked the wind out of me.

"OK, we need to *Macho Man* our way to the Ice House on Decatur!" Cole continued to work the crowd into a frenzy. All you macho men who can carry a queen piggyback or on your shoulders grab one at the door on the way out. They're wearing heels and can't run to the party. We want to run there and show up before any other clubs!"

Everyone was screaming "Yeah, let's go!" and heading for the door. Some very large body builder grabbed me, told me to hike up my dress, and had me ride piggy back on him as he sprinted down the street. The street was filled with guys running or carrying others who couldn't run because of the dresses or high heels they had on. Cole led the charge. When we got to the Ice House, Cole jumped up on the brick railing and yelled, "We need to push down the door!! Show them who the biggest and best macho men are!" My ride put me down and proceeded to charge the overhead metal door with the others. On the second big push it came down, and it fell into the warehouse. The crowd ran over it into the space whooping and hollering. Cole grabbed my hand and pulled me in with him. I looked around and did not see Dante. Once we were inside, I pointed out the room Jiff was in and Cole got a couple of guys to break open the door telling them that is where he thought the bar was. Jiff was in there, seated, and tied to a column. They had come back, found me gone, and roughed him up before tying him up again to the column. I ran to him. "Are you all right. Can you stand up?" Cole and I got him to his feet. By now the crowd was getting restless and wondering where the party was.

Black, Blue and Ratty were looking down on us from a mezzanine office at the other end of the building. I could see the blank, dense look on their faces. Ratty realized the problem.

Cole yelled out, "There! Those guys lied to me about the party! Get em!"

The crowd went after them knocking down the columns and the metal stairs up to the second floor office space. With the lack of support the office started to pull away from the wall.

Ratty and the boys had locked themselves in the office and were working on barricading themselves in when Cole directed the angry crowd at them. Once the mob knocked down the supports, the floor started sagging, and hung precariously twenty feet above the warehouse floor. We could see them through the glass windows trying to find something they could hold onto if the floor fell out from under them. That's when we heard police sirens. The disappointed and unruly crowd started to scatter and all that was left was Jiff, Cole, and me.

I told Cole, "Thanks. You might want to get out of here, I don't want you to get in any trouble."

"I won't. I didn't break in the door, the angry crowd did. I'm here to save you and your friend."

"I think Stan wants to do that." I said nodding in Stan's direction as he ushered in the cops pointing toward me and Jiff.

"Brandy, what's with all the makeup? And, that dress? You look like a . . ." Stan was trailing off the end of the sentence and looking at Cole in the Indian head dress.

"An exotic dancer?" Cole teased finishing

Stan's sentence.

I started making polite introductions while Stan checked out Cole in his loin cloth, feathered head piece, moccasins, and chiseled body. "Stan, this is Cole, I mean, Silas, a friend of the family. Then the rest flew out so fast I just wanted to say it and have it be over. "He hid Isabella and me from Ratty's two guys. They came after me when Jiff helped me escape. Jiff helped me over that wall." I nodded to the wall still looking around to see if any of the roach's friends were looking for him or me. "When those guys came into the club looking for me, Cole and his friends hid us and kept us safe. After that, I called you, and Silas brought the calvary here to get Jiff out." I didn't want all the credit to go to Silas and not recognize Jiff's part of getting me out of the Ice House. Ah, three fragile male egos to juggle, Stan, Silas and Jiff.

"Brandy?" Jiff finally spoke to me. "I didn't realize that was you trying to help me up. Are you okay? That's not your dress. Where's Isabella?" He looked confused.

"Well, by now Isabella has probably had her hair done and is still resting in a very safe place." I said as I smiled at Silas.

Stan took charge and went straight to talk with the police to explain who was who and why we were all here. He headed over to the police captain who had arrived. I was sure Stan was giving information to the police as to who Ratty and his two neanderthals were. I heard one of the policemen saying to Stan, "We need to call the Fire Department in here to get those guys down from there. That's not something we handle. We'll arrest them after the Fire Department gets them down." Oh boy, here we go again.

"I'll call you tomorrow." Stan said to me as the captain went to find an underling to radio the Fire Department. "It seems Dante's partner knows these guys and may have had something to do with your abduction. Dante started following him and followed him into that night club. He lost Joe when the mayhem broke out." As he leaned to kiss me goodbye he said in my ear, "You might want to change out of that getup before you go home. Your parents will think you are working Bourbon Street."

Stan shook Jiff's hand and told him to make sure I got home safely. Then, he went to see if one of the patrol units could give us a ride.

"Let's go back to the club and we'll get your clothes and Isabella." Silas said to me. Stan asked the police captain if one of his officers could give us a lift back to Oz. The captain directed one of his men to take us back to the club.

Once there, Jiff called his father to let him know he was safe and who I was, in case his dad heard anything from the police or on the news.

Then he waited downstairs and ordered drinks for everyone in the club, on him, while I changed upstairs. I thanked everyone who came to my assistance and kissed Lola on the check. "You helped me most of all hiding me under that beautiful head piece. And thanks for letting me wear one of your gowns to the party."

I could swear she blushed. Then she said, "You can thank me by telling me how you found that handsome man."

I gave her the Reader's Digest version from the parade kiss when he knocked my socks off right up to this moment. She was surprised to find out we had just met. Lola thought we were married or engaged. I smiled.

I had a drink with Jiff and asked him in his ear if this place made him nervous. He said, "Why, I'm with you. I like not having any competition from any other guy here." It was my turn to blush.

Cole came down resplendid in full dress. "Is that one of your dad's costumes? It's exquisite." I asked noticing the workmanship and hours it must have taken to construct such a magnificent piece. Then I thought, *Silas, or Cole, how do you pull off a double life like this? How do you keep it separate from family or friends you don't want to know?*

"Yes. You know the Tchoupitoulas Indians?" Cole asked.

"Woozie talks about the costumes all the time

to me. She is always telling me what feathers or sequins she is looking for and where she has to buy them for you. I know you and your dad, or just the men, can work on the costumes. The women aren't allowed."

"Well, you do know about the Indians. The men in my family have been Wild Tchoupitoulas Indians for generations because our heritage is Indian, Black, French, and German. You know, Creole. My granddad was one, and my dad was his spy boy. Then my dad took over from my granddad and I was his spy boy. Every year they start work on a new costume right after Mardi Gras. Tradition has it they wear a costume once. So he never misses the feathers from the ones he has stored in the attic. I help them make the new costumes every year so when they ask me to go get some feathers off a costume, I make sure they never see which one is missing."

The entertainment was beginning and first up was Lola who dedicated a song to Jiff from me. She lip synced *When Will I See You Again?* by the Three Degrees. We laughed and stayed to have another drink in order to decompress from the last two days' events. The bartender brought a go cup filled with water for Isabella who sat on the barstool next to Jiff. When Lola finished, Big Chief grabbed the mike from her and dedicated a song to me from Jiff. The song was *I'm Your Man* by WHAM!. The entire bar joined in singing, turning to the person they were with.

When we were ready to leave, Cole called us a taxi and put us in it at the door. He handed us two drinks in go cups. "About my mother," he started to say something but I cut him off.

"What happens in Oz, stays in Oz." I kissed him on the cheek and Jiff shook his hand. It was about eleven P.M. when we got into the taxi. I said to Jiff, "Well, on our first date you got shot, and on our second date we got kidnapped. I can't wait to see what we do on our third date." Jiff sat there smiling at me from ear to ear. "This is a terrible start. Why are you smiling?" I asked him.

"We're dating, you just said it. I'd like to show the most incredible woman I've ever met my appreciation for what you did for me and Isabella. Let me take you to dinner wherever you want. Pick your favorite place or anyplace you want to go. Name it." Jiff said taking my hand.

"Well in that case, I want to go to College Inn. It's where you offered to take me on our first official date. We can sit outside like we planned with Isabella. I might even bring Meaux."

"It's a date. I'll pick you up tomorrow evening at seven P.M. I need to go home and get some rest." he said.

"Me too." I said just as the taxi stopped in front of my parents' house. I gave Isabella a kiss on top of her head and she wagged her short little tail and gave me a doggy smile. Only God knows what was waiting inside with my parents so I diplomatically suggested he wait to meet them when he came to pick me up for our dinner date. Mom and Dad were about to hear enough surprises with the station wagon stolen, the kidnapping and the rescue. I thought the new boyfriend needed to be on tomorrow's agenda.

He got out the cab, walked to my side and opened the door for me. He saw me to my front door, and kissed me goodnight. The second kiss did not disappoint. I don't know how long we stood there but like the first kiss, everything stopped, my leg bent at the knee like in a romantic movie scene. He put his hand behind my head and whispered in my ear, "Until tomorrow." Fireworks were going off in my head. He waited until I walked into my house and closed the door before getting into the taxi to leave. Julia said his dad was a gentleman. It seems the apple didn't fall far from the tree.

I closed the front door and leaned on it. I finally had a moment to myself and my roller coaster emotions. One second I had butterflies in my stomach and the next it was in knots thinking of Dante and everything that had transpired over the last forty-eight hours. My face felt hot. One second I felt furious at Dante for keeping things from me, and in the next, I was almost relieved. The information about him had me angry, hurt, and sympathetic all at once. Everything was spinning around, in and out of focus. Why didn't he trust me enough to tell me, why did he lead me to think we were in a committed relationship? I second guessed myself. Did I miss some obvious signals? Should I have picked up on the fact that he was so non-committal? It did explain a few things, like why we didn't move forward in our relationship, like why we had not set a wedding date, why we always seemed more like brother and sister, why he was protective of me but not emotionally available to me. I could see why he didn't want anyone to know—being on the police force, growing up in our male-dominated neighborhood, having five brothers. That made me wonder if one of his brothers knew and was keeping his secret from me too. I was sure if he came out to his family, they would understand— or not. What was I thinking? No way, who was I kidding? All I kept coming back to was how in the world did he keep his secret in this city? Everybody knows someone everybody else knows. This was a keg of dynamite with a fuse, and someone like Julia had a match.

I grew up in his family as much as my own. I had to think Miss Ruth, Dante's mother, would just want him to be happy. Well, she wanted him to be happy *and* married to me, *and* have lots of grandkids for her to spoil. This was a giant cluster if ever there was one.

This was a lot to digest, and I needed time. I began to question my own sense of judgment. In the last forty-eight hours my life derailed at the parade and shot me into a parallel universe with Julia, Club Bare Minimum, Duck Man, Charity Hospital, Oz, Stan, and Jiff. I didn't feel confident in my ability to make a good call.

I needed to speak to Dante to come to terms with this and let him know I still loved him and I knew he loved me. We were just not lovers. He was my best friend and nothing would ever change that. His secret would be safe with me as long as he wanted it to be. I had to let him know that I would love him forever, no matter what. I was Irish, I could take a secret to the grave. My head was spinning, and I needed sleep.

I walked through my apartment door at the rear and heard my father shout up the hall, "Brandy, is that you?" Oh boy, this should be fun on three hours sleep over the last two days.

"Yeah, Dad, it's me."

"We're in the kitchen." They were both up and in the kitchen. Great. I knew explaining to him would not be a big problem except where the station wagon was concerned. My mother? Different story. When I got to the kitchen, he and my mother were sitting at the table. They were sitting across from each other and there was a letter in the middle of the table between them. He pulled a chair out for me. They sat there and just looked at me. They each had a cup of coffee and appeared to have been up all night worrying. My dad poured me a cup and set it on the table.

"We have been so worried when you didn't come home, and you left that note about your mom's station wagon. Then, this morning, a courier came in person and delivered this letter from a law office for you."

He handed me a letter from the Law Offices of Heinkel and Heinkel, and it was addressed to me. Then, he and my mother held hands across the table like they were waiting for bad news.

"About the station wagon, I'm so sorry to have to tell you how I found it."

"Left in the project and burned up." Dad said.

"Yes, how did you know?" I asked.

"Dante told us when he saw the police report on it," Mom added. She didn't want me to think my dad was a psychic.

"Really, from a police report?" I thought, *and not the Fire Department?* "Oh Mom, I'm so sorry. These two guys were following me and stole it from where I parked outside of Charity's emergency entrance. I went to see a friend who got shot. I have money saved, I'll buy you another car. I promise."

"Who got shot? You were in Charity? Did you get shot at? What were you doing around people shooting guns at a party?" I never heard my mother sound so concerned about my welfare and not accuse me of making someone shoot at me. I guess she still thought I went to a party with Julia.

"Is that why you are in trouble? Is that why these lawyers are sending you papers?" asked Dad.

"I'm not in any trouble. Papers? What?" I opened the letter in my hand and inside was a check for One Thousand Dollars made out to Schnauzer Rescue and me. The note said, *Thank you for saving my son and Isabella. This is for rescue. Call a car rental company and get what you need until you get a new car and let my office know. I want to pay for the rental and a new car.* It was signed by Geoffrey A. Heinkel – Heinkel Law Firm.

"Mom, did you forget Dante carries a gun?" I asked her, somewhat distracted by the letter from Jiff's father along with the check.

"What's in that letter? Are you in some kind of trouble?" asked my dad.

"It is a very long story and I need to get some sleep. I'm okay and I will buy you another car with the money I have saved."

I knew I wouldn't let Mr. Heinkel buy me a car, but he sure could donate to rescue. "I'm not in trouble. This is a donation for saving someone's dog, a Schnauzer."

"Brandy, you did me a favor. That station wagon served our family well, but it wasn't going to last much longer. It was on its last leg. You didn't notice how much oil it was burning? It needed a new engine. It was too old to spend any more money on. I kept putting off looking for new car. Your dad is going to take me shopping for a new one on Ash Wednesday, the day after Mardi Gras. I'm getting a brand new car and the insurance money will help pay for it." My mother sounded and looked almost happy. Well, as happy as I had ever seen her.

"That station wagon marks the end of an era," my dad said.

"Error. End of an error." I corrected him, and we all laughed. They both looked less tired than when I first got home.

My mother pulled at my hair and came away with a small yellow feather. "Where did you get this?"

"It's a long story," I said yawning. "I will tell you about it tomorrow. I need some sleep." I got up from the kitchen table and headed toward my apartment at the rear of the house. Looking at my watch I tried to figure out if my date was tonight or tomorrow night. I grabbed a go cup and filled it with ice water. Over my shoulder I said to them, "I have a date tonight at seven o'clock. It's with the guy I kissed at the parade. I think y'all will like him. His dad sent me this." I left the envelope on the kitchen table for them to read, and then headed to the mattress ball.

"Oh, and I'm moving in with Suzanne. We're going to share an apartment. Don't worry . . . I'm taking all the dogs. Goodnight."

The End

About the Author

Colleen Mooney was born and raised in New Orleans, Louisiana, where she lives with her husband and three Schnauzers, Meaux Jeaux, MoonPie and Mauser the Schnauzer, aka Maus. She graduated from Loyola University of the South and has lived in Birmingham, Alabama, New York City, Madison, New Jersey and Atlanta, Georgia. She has been a volunteer for Schnauzer Rescue of Louisiana in the New Orleans area for over twelve years and has placed approximately 225 abandoned, surrendered or stray Schnauzers. If you are interested in learning more about New Orleans or Schnauzers, please contact her at one of the following:

email: colleen@colleenmooney.com

Website: www.colleenmooney.com

Facebook: facebook.com/ColleenMooneyAuthor

Twitter: twitter.com/mooney_colleen

Read the next book from The New Orleans Go Cup Chronicles series, DEAD and BREAKFAST

Dead & Breakfast

From The New Orleans Go Cup Chronicles

"BRANDY, GET OVER here now. There's a dead guy in one of my guest rooms." Julia Richard dropped that bomb on me when she called at 5:55 a.m., and then simply hung up.

I arrived at The Canal Street Guest House at 6:20 a.m. on the humid April morning, let myself in downstairs through the kitchen at the rear of the building—I knew the four-digit code on the back door designed for guests to let themselves in after 11 p.m. when Julia locked the front doors—and headed upstairs.

I found Julia standing over a dead man in one of her guest rooms. She looked like she just stepped out of the shower, and was dressed for the day. One might think this her normal appearance, except for her blood-covered hands. The dead guy was nude, facedown, lying diagonally across an antique four-poster bed. One leg of the bed was broken, causing the bed and body to tilt headfirst at a forty-five degree angle. He had a gash in the back of his skull. Blood was everywhere, all over the sheets and the Oriental rug on the floor. Handprints and fingerprints of blood were on the phone, the bedposts and the dead guy. Looking around the room, I couldn't help but wonder why I would be the first person thought of after witnessing this tableau.

My name is Brandy Alexander and I have lived in New Orleans all my life. My Dad and his rogue brother, Uncle Andrew, thought of my name while in a bar waiting for me to arrive at Baptist Hospital. The more they drank, the more they convinced themselves that a great New Orleans name for a girl with the last name Alexander would be Brandy. So, just like that, my Dad inked it on the birth certificate before my mother had a say, and she has never missed an opportunity to remind me that I have a stripper's name ever since, like I had something to do with it. My burden in life is a southern, Catholic mother who believes that I am somehow responsible for everything that goes wrong in the world.

"I can't believe this is happening on the first day I'm open," Julia whined when I walked in.

"I can't believe it's happening at all. Have you called the police or just me?" My stomach was knotting up as I mentally indexed things I touched in the mansion during recent visits here to help

Julia.

"No, Brandy, do not call the police," she said without taking her eyes off the dead guy.

"Who do you want to call? It's a dead body. What do you think you can do with it? Sneak it over the fence into the cemetery next door? You have to call the police." I froze in mid-reach for the phone in the room when I again saw that it was covered in bloody fingerprints. "Is this the phone you used to call me?"

"Yes," she stood in front of it blocking me from picking it up.

"You didn't kill him, did you?" I started to rub my temples with my index fingers hoping to jumpstart my thinking power.

"No. I don't think so."

"You don't think so? What do you mean?"

"I don't remember much of last night after we got into this room. He opened a bottle of wine he had brought with him and poured us each a glass. I remember I started feeling frisky, then it's all a blur."

"Julia, how much of the wine did you drink? Maybe he slipped you something. Where are the glasses and the bottle?"

"Well, the bottle and the glasses were over there on that tray table or maybe on the dresser, I think. I don't remember how much of it I drank."

"Where are they now? Did you bring them

downstairs?" I asked, looking around. The bottle and the glasses were not in the room.

"No. I don't remember moving them." Julia's eyes never left the dead guy.

"Where is the wine bottle?" I asked her again.

"I don't know. I really didn't want any more to drink but he insisted saying it was a fantastic bottle a friend had given him. I don't remember much after a few sips of that wine. Oh, God, this is going to ruin my business." Julia looked deflated. Her normal perfect posture was transformed as her head and shoulders slumped forward like an old woman.

"If you don't call the police, this is going to ruin your life, along with mine. I'm not going to be an accessory to murder. Don't touch anything else. I'm guessing these are all your fingerprints in his blood or did you find some here and decided to add yours to the collection?" I asked, still looking around the room. It was as if the room had been ransacked; bedding pulled off at the corners, pillows everywhere, and a suitcase sitting on the luggage rack, its contents spilling onto the floor. Clothes were strewn from one end of the room to the other, a man's clothes-shirt, pants, underwear, shoes-along with a pair of woman's black stockings and a black lace garter belt. A worn hard shell guitar case was covered in band decals for a group that played throughout the south called The Levee

Men and one "See Rock City" decal. It was unopened on the floor and sat next to the suitcase.

The floor-to-ceiling windows were all the way open and the lace curtains billowed out to the veranda. The windows opened high enough so that I could have ducked my head and walked out onto the balcony. Someone shorter than my 5'8" height could walk in and out like a doorway. I could see the sheer curtains waving around the bistro table and two chairs set up out there. An enormous oak tree covered the entire front of the house and most of the porch, making it feel like you were sitting in a tree house.

"The ones in the blood are mine." Julia's words brought my attention back inside. Her eyes were fixed on the body as she spoke to me, "My fingerprints are going to be all over this room. I did the cleaning before this guy checked in."

"How is it you have blood all over your hands? Is it yours or his?" I asked cautiously.

"I thought he was still alive when I found him. I shook him to try to wake him."

"You moved the body?" The police were going to love this fact.

"Yes, but I put him back exactly like I found him."

"Oh boy, with his blood on you, this looks like you did it," I let slip before I realized the effect it would have on her. She went pale and looked at her hands covered in blood as if she just noticed it. "Did you hear or see anything?"

"Uh, uh." Julia struggled with an answer.

"It looks like he put up a fight from the condition this room is in. Did you fight this guy off? That bed is going to need serious restoration." I said, looking at the forty-five degree lean of the antique bedframe. My eyes scanned the room again and stopped on the black lace thong hanging from the chandelier. "Yours?"

"Yes, I guess they are," Julia answered and went pale.

"You guess they are? Was there a third person in your party?" I crossed my arms and shifted into a more comfortable stance. "Go on."

"We, uh, were having a good time, uh, and then, uh, the last thing I sort of remember was the bed broke. We just continued with the uh, sex, uh, until, uh," she trailed off, completely out of "uhs." Her voice quivered, then her body buckled at the knees causing her shoulders, neck and head to roll. She looked like she was doing a full body impression of the wave that goes around a stadium at a football game. I caught her by the arm to steady her.

I wasn't going to get any information from her if she kept staring at the guy. I ushered her out of the room.

"I'm guessing the blood rushing to his head is

not what killed him."

"Maybe I did kill him and I just don't remember. I can't remember much of anything after we got in bed. I mean, I remember getting frisky, then the bed broke but everything sort of goes black from there. I know we were getting friendly, but I'm not sure we actually did it."

"Don't ever say that again, the part where you think you might have killed him, not the part where you're not sure you did it. Well, don't say that either. If you killed him, and I don't think you did, I know you would remember. Do you think you were drugged?

"I don't know," she whispered as if she couldn't find the energy to talk.

"We had better go to the kitchen and call the police. Then I want you to tell me everything you remember from the moment this guy checked in. The police are going to ask you, so it would be good for you to start remembering. I'll stay with you and help you anyway I can." This was a cluster if I ever saw one.

Julia had opened a hospitality business in New Orleans. She knew nothing about guest houses or how to manage a hotel and of all places to buy, she chose a former funeral home and crematory on Canal Street. Canal Street, the city's widest boulevard, runs across the entire city of New Orleans, from the Mississippi River to Lake

Pontchartrain. The streetcar line makes a stop steps away from Julia's front door. This Victorian, was built in the late 1800s as a private residence, rivaled many of the city's grand mansions, and later was turned into a funeral home since it was located at the edge of the city limits where people came to bury their loved ones. Now, it is surrounded by cemeteries on two sides, around the corner and across the street. It has a columned portico for its entrance and a Porte cochere. The Porte cochere was formerly the side entrance used to allow horse drawn carriages arriving with passengers. When the building had served as a funeral home this entrance was used to accommodate the coroner's van dropping off or hearses picking up the dearly, or not so dearly, departed on their very short ride to their final resting place, next door. Julia's guest house now used this side entrance to shelter guests from rain as they arrived or departed in limousines or taxis.

Julia had been trying to divorce her husband S.J., but they were at a standoff on who was going to pay for the legal fees. This ended when he suddenly died leaving Julia a widow rather than a divorcee. After his death, she'd found suitcases of money he had hidden at a storage facility, presumably trying to keep it out of the divorce settlement. Now it was legally hers. Today, thanks to that money, she was opening the doors at the renovated guest house and this guy had the audacity to die in one of her rooms.

We went downstairs to the kitchen at the rear of the building where I had earlier let myself in. Julia went to the sink and washed the blood off her hands.

The kitchen was a large room and all the appliances were top of the line. Everything was commercial size, a Subzero refrigerator and freezer, a Viking stove, two sets of triple sinks along miles of countertops with enough Carrera marble to rebuild Italy. Julia had done a brilliant job renovating the abandoned mansion, adding modern conveniences along with beautiful, comfortable antiques. The woman had great taste and after finding the cash S.J. had been holding out on her, she had enough money to buy the best. I told Julia to thank God every day her divorce was never finalized.

"The longer we wait to call the police the worse this will get." I went to the phone on the wall and dialed 9-1-1. I told them the name of the guest house, the address and that there was a dead guy here in one of the guest rooms.

The dispatcher asked if there was anyone hurt or in need of an ambulance.

"Does dead count as hurt?" I asked.

After she paused long enough to convey annoyance or indifference—I mean we are talking about a New Orleans city worker—she said, "That's a no for an ambulance, then. Don't let anyone leave. A police car will be there…shortly." I realized she hung up when I heard the dial tone.

"Start at the beginning and don't leave anything out, but make it quick, the police will be here shortly." I did the finger quotes around shortly but Julia wasn't in the right frame of mind to appreciate sarcasm. "Is anyone else in the building? Other guests, housekeepers, workers?"

"No, no, just him. He told me he came here to play at the Jazz Festival this weekend. He arrived a day early to see some of his favorite New Orleans places before the rest of his band gets in town. Oh God, some of the band members coming in from out of town are suppose to check in later today. What am I going to tell them?"

"Let's worry about what you are going to tell the police. So, how did you end up in his room?"

"After he checked in, he asked me to call him a cab to go to the French Quarter. Oh God!" Julia started wringing her hands.

"What?"

"I took him to the Napoleon House where my friend Andy is a bartender. He was working last night and will remember us having drinks till about midnight."

"Sit down. Take a breath and just tell me everything you know or remember from the beginning. Start with his name."

Julia sat staring at the wall across from her seat at the kitchen island. I went about finding coffee and putting on a pot. After I prodded Julia a few times to stay calm, collect her thoughts and start at the beginning, she finally looked at me.

When the automatic coffee maker made the swooshing hiss with the three beeps alerting caffeine-addicted individuals, such as myself, that it was ready I poured us each a cup. I found a bottle of Jameson's in the cabinet hidden behind a pound of Café du Monde coffee and chicory, powdered creamer, and a box of sugar free packets—Julia's private stash. I added a generous splash of the whiskey to her coffee to help take the edge off her nerves. I was tempted to give myself a splash but it was still a little early and it was a work day for me, even though it didn't look like I'd be getting much done today.

"His name is Guitarzan."

"This is no time for jokes."

"No, he said his friends in the band called him Guitarzan."

"Is he in the jungle band with Jane and the Monkey?" I asked, trying to make her laugh and lighten the situation at hand. Julia ignored me.

"I have been working non-stop on this place getting it ready to open and I needed a break. After he checked in, he came back downstairs and asked me to call him a cab. He wanted to go to the French Quarter. Then he asked if I'd like to go with him and have a drink, so I said yes." Julia's voice was getting shaky again.

"What's his real name, Julia?" I asked, starting at square one.

"Oh, yeah, his real name is Gervais St. Germain."

"Okay." "Guitarzan" was making sense now. "Where did y'all go?"

"I called a cab and we took it to the Napoleon House, like I said. After our drinks, we walked around Jackson Square and I called another cab to bring us back here. I'm guessing we got back here around 1:00 to 1:30 a.m."

"So, there are two cab drivers out there who saw you with him last night," I said.

She burst into tears. Through tears and sniffles, she rendered the rest of the evening for me. They'd returned and had a nightcap in the salon. Julia went to his room, to make sure he had enough towels. *Who was she kidding?* Anyway, one thing led to another and after a night of whoopee she woke up with a killer headache.

"I realized the bed was broken and figured we'd had a real fun night of it. I felt so bad when I woke up, way worse than I should have felt for only having a couple of drinks. I slipped out the bed so I wouldn't wake him and left his room. I went to shower to help wake myself up. I was in the shower a while and still felt like I couldn't wake up. After my shower I went downstairs to make him breakfast and prep food for the other guests arriving later that day. When I brought the tray up to his room...I found him...like that. I didn't know, I didn't see him like that when I sneaked out of his room earlier. It was still dark."

She told me she'd dropped the tray of food when she saw all the blood. It was still there, all over the floor, just inside the door.

"That must have been a wild night if you two broke the bed," I said.

"Yeah, I guess so, even though I don't remember much after we got into this room," Julia said.

"So, what did y'all talk about last night? Did he have friends here or was he supposed to meet someone else here, since he came in a day early?" I asked her.

"I don't know," she blubbered.

"Anything else? Can you remember anything else about him?"

"He wore a purple stone, I think was an amethyst, on a black leather cord like a necklace. I didn't see it on him when I found him this morning and I know he had it on last night when we went out. He said he never took it off."

"Did he get any messages? Check and see if anyone called looking for him."

We went into the hallway where the answering machine sat on a leggy, gold leafed antique reception desk. It was blinking and indicated there were new messages. We hit play and the first one was a woman's voice saying she knew Gervais St. Germain was checking in. She didn't leave a name but left her number and said, "tell him to call me." The second caller was a hang up and left no message, but the caller did breathe heavily into the phone for a few seconds.

"That's the same weirdo who has called here several times and always just hangs up. It's always from a blocked number," Julia said after she replayed the messages and wrote down the phone number from the first on a scrap of paper on the desk.

I looked at my watch.

"Where are the police?" she asked. Almost thirty minutes had passed since I phoned.

"You should offer coffee and donuts for all cops in this precinct as part of your marketing. Then, they will keep an eye on the place," I said. "Or they might show up faster if you call in for help."

"Now you tell me."

Y Y Y

I LOVE KING Cakes and I don't need to be stressed to eat a whole one by myself, although I would have used that as an excuse this morning. My stomach was doing flips while we waited and I tried to get more information out of Julia. I didn't relish seeing whoever showed up from the New Orleans Police Department. I was bound to know them since my ex boyfriend was a cop. I couldn't stop craving king cake.

King Cakes are braided cinnamon rolls shaped into hollow circles covered in purple, green and gold sugared icing, the colors of Mardi Gras. There is a plastic doll hidden inside and the person who gets the piece with the doll has certain obligations while enjoying the reign as king or queen for the duration of the party. These cakes can only be found in New Orleans during the weeks of Mardi Gras season, from the Catholic Feast of the Epiphany through Fat Tuesday or until Ash Wednesday starts. They are the energy food that fuels parade goers. The sugar alone gives you enough energy to maintain the grueling pace needed for weeks dedicated to parading, partying and drinking. It is my official food of Carnival. I could have used a piece right now to help me cope with this mess with Julia. Available everywhere during Mardi Gras, one or two bakeries ship them year round, so I can special order one any time my stress-o-meter screams for some of that sugary saboteur to my normally healthy diet. I was thinking about calling to order one.

Two cups of coffee later, another splash of Jameson for Julia, and my craving for King Cake totally unsatisfied, we still waited. It had been over an hour since I called the police.

While we waited, Julia and I discussed more of what had happened and how much she didn't know about the man who was now dead in her guest room. I told her that when the police arrived she should tell the truth, as much as she could remember, and if she didn't know something, say she didn't know it. If, for any reason, they decided to take her in for questioning, I told her to tell them she wanted a lawyer and not to say another thing. I knew her calling me before she called the police was going to be a problem, but I didn't think it would be a big problem until an unmarked police car, in typical fashion—long after the immediate crises was over—screamed up to the front of the building, siren wailing, lights flashing and brakes screeching as it slammed to a stop. A Ford Crown Vic, the police department's unmarked car of choice arrived, flashed the blue dashboard light and pinched off a single bloop on the siren by way of announcing themselves. The tinted windows didn't allow me to see who was inside. No one got out immediately in spite of their arrival at breakneck speed. When the driver and passenger doors finally opened, a male and female officer got out of the car. I knew this was not going to go well. Julia's chances would have been fine had the first cop on the scene not been my childhood sweetheart and ex-boyfriend, Dante Deedler.

Dante and his new partner.

During the initial aftermath of our breakup, I thought—or was led to believe—that Dante was gay, and that was why our relationship was going nowhere. Local gossip from the old neighborhood where we grew up next door to each other was happy to update me on this recent development…the new partner was also his new girlfriend.

Chapter Two

JULIA AND I walked out to the front porch to meet the police. Dante strode up the steps and introduced himself as Detective Deedler, as if we didn't know him. His previous partner, Joe, had been arrested and was awaiting trial for his involvement in the oil lease scam I'd stumbled into after I kissed the guy I was now dating in a Mardi Gras parade a couple of months ago. Dante and I had not spoken since.

Dante's partner stuck her arm straight out, like a karate punch, holding her shield in my face. I had to lean my head back to read it. It said Z. Hanky. Z stood for Zide, or so the twenty-four-hour satellite operated, neighborhood rumor mill detected and texted me within seconds of obtaining the info. In the past, I would have had to wait for a call over a secure line or a face-to-face meeting at a predetermined locale, like my favorite bar on St. Charles Avenue. The busybody hotline also passed along the useless but interesting tidbit that Dante's police unit had given her a nickname.

My face was fighting the urge to burst out laughing at the thought of the other cops calling her Hanky Panky. Dante appeared to be in an ill humor.

"What happened?" he asked, opening his notebook without looking at either of us.

I looked at Julia. She was standing there as if in a trance.

"Julia?" Dante asked not looking up from the notebook. His partner put one hand on her gun, the other on her nightstick and stared at me. I guess I didn't need to introduce myself.

Julia turned around, walked inside and started up the steps. I waited for Dante and Officer Friendly to follow. Dante looked up and gave me an after-you gesture. Detective Hanky followed me with Dante bringing up the rear. We all trudged up the stairs to the second floor guest room. I thought the dead guy looked more ghostlike now. I'm sure rigor was setting in.

This was the first time I had seen Dante in a couple of months. During Mardi Gras a couple of months ago I was told by the bartender of a popular gay club in the French Quarter that he saw Dante in there often, in plain clothes. I thought I had it on good authority that Dante was gay. Turns out, Dante was undercover so I had bad information on him being homosexual. The good information someone shared was that he was pretty ticked off at me for thinking this. After-wards, Dante and I mutually agreed it would be best if we dated other people. By mutually agreed, I mean, I decided to date other people and Dante ignored me and just went about his business as usual. It didn't help that we'd both lived with our parents right next door to each other since birth, and I was going to be under the magnifying glass every time I had a date. Someone was always ready to report to one of us about the goings on of the other. So, I moved out of the family home and into an apartment with Suzanne, another child-hood friend from the neighborhood. Suzanne did know when to keep her mouth shut and stayed clear of the gossip rodeo. Over the last couple of months, life had become a roller coaster of adjustments. Seeing Dante for the first time since the move and breakup was harder than I thought it would be, especially seeing him with his new girlfriend at a murder scene.

Julia took a small step over the threshold into the room and immediately moved along the wall plastering herself against it. She stood staring at the body.

Dante's partner leaned over the body to check for a pulse. She looked back at him and shook her head. That's when I noticed her extra wide backside. From the rear she looked as wide as she was tall and I'm not counting the holster with all their police stuff—gun, flashlight, handcuffs, radio—just her big butt filling out a pair of ill-fitting polyester uniform pants. I was feeling tall and thin, and stood up a little straighter.

"Julia, how do you know the victim?" Dante asked her, walking around the room making notes of the havoc, the food on the floor, the disarranged furniture, the man's clothes and the lady things.

"I. He. He's a guest," she mumbled.

"Did you get a name and address when he checked in?"

"His name is Gervais St. Germain and he said he's from here but travels a lot with the band he plays with, The Levee Men. He doesn't keep an apartment here anymore," she answered.

Oh good, I had hoped she would leave off the 'Guitarzan' part.

"Do you know if he has any aliases, nicknames, something else he could have been known by?" Dante asked.

Here goes.

"He told me the band guys called him Guitar-zan."

"So are you the gymnast or was Guitarzan here swinging from the chandelier?" asked Detective Hanky, nodding toward the ceiling.

No wonder Dante liked her. She was a riot.

"When did you last see him?" Dante looked directly at Julia when he asked.

"Maybe 5:00 or 5:15 this morning when I woke up and went down to get us some juice and rolls," Julia said. This got a raised eyebrow from the partner-girlfriend wearing, men's polyester uniform pants.

"What is your relationship with this man?" Dante was doing the interrogation while big butt was looking through the dead guy's suitcase for a wallet or an I.D.

"I don't have a relationship with him. He, he just checked in last night."

"How is it you last saw him at 5:15 this morning?" he asked, looking right at the chandelier with the lace thong hanging from it.

"How do you think?" I answered, trying to save her some embarrassment.

"I need Julia to answer the questions, unless of course," he said, pausing and giving me a steely look, "you were here, too."

I gave him one of the stares I'd inherited from my mother and he turned his attentions back to Julia.

"I slept in here with him," Julia stated as if it took her last breath. She looked unstable on her feet.

"Who else is registered here as a guest? We'll need a list of their names along with all your staff, and anyone that comes and goes." Dante cast a sideways look in my direction.

"The registered guests are arriving later today," Julia said.

"Where are they?" asked Hanky.

"What part of 'arriving later today' makes you think we know where they are now?" I was immediately sorry I'd mouthed off and air fingered the quotes.

Dante looked like he was going to explode, so he busied himself walking around the room taking notes. He stopped and looked at the bloody phone and the bloody handprints on the body. He looked at Julia and asked, "Are these yours?"

She nodded.

"Julia Richard you need to come with us for questioning," Hanky said, taking Julia by the arm. Julia pushed her hands off her. Hanky immediately cuffed her and started to escort Julia out of the room.

"Is she under arrest?" I asked. Hanky ignored me and Dante was calling in a homicide over the police radio, asking forensics to come to the address to meet Officer Hanky. "I think Julia should consult with an attorney before she answers any questions." To Julia, I added, "I'll call Stan and see if he can meet you." Stan was an old mutual friend and attorney. Dante and I had grown up with him.

I followed behind Hanky with Julia and in front of Dante as we walked down the magnificent stairway Julia had spent a fortune to renovate. The width of the grand old Victorian staircase allowed for Hanky to walk side by side with Julia. We stopped at the front leaded glass doors under the fan window.

"You need to come with us, too," Dante said without looking at me.

"Really, Dante? Are we under arrest? What am I under arrest for?" I really didn't want to be left alone with Detective Wide Side, so being arrested had some appeal.

Hanky never let go of Julia the entire way down the brick entry steps as they left the guest house. "We'll let you know after you answer a few questions." Dante put his hand on Julia's head and guided her into the back seat of the police car.

"Dante, please, can you drive me and my car to the station?" I was right in his face when he stood up closing the door to the squad car. I sounded pitiful whining the question.

He paused and told Detective Hanky to drive the squad car with Julia while he waited for forensics. Then he said he would drive my car and me the precinct. I thought I saw Hanky Panky going for her gun to shoot me on the spot, but Dante stepped between us and spun me around. He pushed me ahead of him back up the steps into the bed and breakfast.

Chapter Three

D ANTE FOLLOWED ME back inside the Canal Street Guest House and told me not to touch anything. The strong smell of the coffee I'd brewed still hung in the air. It was a strong coffee and chicory blend like Dante's mother always brewed early in the morning for her husband and boys before they left for work or school. She would set it up the night before and put it on a timer so it would be ready for them when they got up. Dante was always the first one up. The aroma would drift from her kitchen across the narrow alley between our houses right into my bedroom. It was better than an alarm clock. I closed my eyes thinking of those mornings. Dante would pour us each a steaming cup and come over to sit with me on my front porch. He did this every morning before work and before anyone else was stirring in either house. We would talk about our plans for the day and plan to meet someplace after work. We would meet at either The Columns Hotel to sit out on the veranda or at The Napoleon House, my personal favorite in the French Quarter. We would have a drink and compare what really happened during the day as compared to what we thought would happen over coffee. Mornings were the only time we ever spent truly alone and the smell of the coffee reminded me of how secure I felt talking and sharing my day with him before anyone else was up. I had thought one day after we were married we would sit on our own porch having coffee discussing the three boys I dreamed of having, their little league schedules, having king cake parties and growing old together. We would wake up early and plan who would take the boys to school and who would pick them up, who would get them to their games or dancing school if I had a girl. Dante and I would cook dinner together and we would all eat every day at the same time before he would go off to help our children with their homework. I would press their uniforms and get their lunches ready for the next day. I would put a little surprise in them like a candy or note encouraging them if there was a test or tryouts after school that day. I would make Dante's lunch and tuck a love note in with his sandwich. I would tell my husband how happy I was with him and put a lipstick kiss on it. I would add, 'Be careful and come home to me tonight' on every note. That was what I thought my life would be like.

I wondered what had happened to the happy little kids who grew up next door to each other, played every day at recess and after school. We shared childhood confidences, dreams and secrets. He was my first love, my first kiss, the first boy I danced with and my only boyfriend for most of my life. He was my first love but I guess I was only his childhood friend. Like a good southern, Irish Catholic girl I waited for Dante to bring up our future and marriage. I waited and waited. I guess we didn't share the expectation both families had for us to get married, live on the same block and have a boatload of grandkids for them.

When he left for the military, I waited for him. He didn't ask me to wait, he just kissed me on the cheek and said, "I'll miss you. I'll be back" when I stood with him at the railway station. He probably thought I'd finally move on without him here. I thought he enlisted to get away from me or he would rather be shot at than marry me. He wrote to me but never said he loved me or he missed me. He said he missed home.

He missed home, not me.

I decided to wait for him thinking when he came back we would move on with our lives, together or apart, but, at least I would have an answer. I stayed and lived at home with my parents who happened to be right next door to Dante's parents and four brothers. I had both families keeping an eye on me. We never discussed our feelings for one another, we just heard what our parents said we felt for each other, how we were expected to live our lives together. No one asked us, and we didn't ask each other. He must have hated me for the choreographed life our parents mapped out. I had to wait for him. I had to be right there, in his face when he came back, smothering him along with our parents. Then, to top it all off, when I did kiss someone at a parade, it was right in front of him.

It really didn't endear me to him when I heard, incorrectly, he was gay. Thinking he was gay seemed to explain a lot. Now that he doesn't see me everyday, he can act the way he really feels and I deserve it. He seems happy with his new girlfriend, his new life. I bet he does want to arrest me and lock me up so he won't have to ever look at me again. I wish it had been different when I kissed Jiff at the parade, but I couldn't control how that happened. I wish it had been different so we would at least still be friends.

I waited for him to read me my rights and handcuff me. "Can I sit down?" When I turned around, he was in my face.

"Do what you want." He didn't move.

"So how long have you and Hanky Panky been dating?" I asked trying to lighten the mood and ease the tension I could slice with a knife.

However, it came out all wrong. I sounded snippy and catty, like a jealous ex-girlfriend.

"What made you think I was gay?" he asked, deliberately moving closer with each word, causing me to take an equal number of steps backward.

"I don't know. I mean, now I know I had wrong information. I, uh, guess it's because our relationship wasn't physical or romantic. I didn't see it-us-going anywhere." I was being honest. I inched backwards and got a tight feeling in my stomach from him invading my personal space.

"I bought you a ring. I was waiting on you to set a date."

"How was I supposed to know that? You didn't say anything. Dante, our relationship was stuck in neutral. We were more like friends, not lovers. We never talked about getting married. Our parents did."

"I was waiting on you to bring it up." He continued to move into me until my back was up against a wall.

"You were waiting on me to bring it up?" I couldn't believe what I was hearing. "I think that was your job." Then, he was so close to my face I couldn't focus on him, so I closed my eyes.

He grabbed my hands, laced his fingers through mine and pushed my arms up over my head, forcing them against the wall. I wanted to slap him but couldn't free my hands. He stepped into me until his body totally pressed against mine. Our knees were touching. Dante had never handled me like this. The sensation of his body so close and completely all over me stirred both fear and arousal at the same time. His mouth was all over my neck, then my face and when he moved onto my mouth, I kissed him back. Then he let go of me and pushed himself away.

"Is that physical enough for you?" He stormed off to the kitchen.

I stood there waiting for the heat to leave my body.

CPSIA information can be obtained
at www.ICGtesting.com
Printed in the USA
LVHW080907240120
PP15638200001B/5